HOLOGRAM

For previews and information about the author, visit Dayenelissbooks on Instagram.

This is a work of fiction, any resemblance to actual people, living or dead, or actual events is purely coincidental.

HOLOGRAM

THERE'S A PROPORTIONAL PRICE TO PAY FOR EACH ADVANCE

WRITTEN BY:
DAYENELISS PEREZ

"MY FATHER WORKED TOO HARD FOR ME NOT TO BE GREAT..."

BY: DAYENELISS PEREZ

Hologram

CHAPTER 1

I felt confused while looking at the board with suspects in Shelly's case. I glanced out the window at my brother Danny. Signaling him to come. Danny came to the room, "Any update?."

"No, not yet," I replied, pointing at Michael Mango's picture.

Danny looked at me with a smile "What kind of last name is Mango?"

As usual, my brother has a spark for humor in the most serious of moments."

I rolled my eyes. "Our job is not to criticize people's names."

Max opened the door and stuck his head inside the room.

"Derick wants to see you both in his office."

Danny and I gazed at each other with curiosity. Walking out of the door. I saw Detective Derrick's office curtains closed. Seeing the curtains closed is quite off, he usually has his curtains open. Danny opened the door. Entering the office, Derick looked worried as he sat in his brown leather chair. As soon as we came in, he looked up with urgency, as if he was in a hurry. He stood up abruptly, walked over to me and Danny, and shook our hands.

"Please take a seat," showing the chairs.

Danny and I took a seat. Derick immediately walked towards the side of the table where all the important equipment was carefully stacked and turned on his projector. In a flash appeared a picture of the governor's family, zooming to the little boy.

"This is Cole, son of Governor Walter." "He went missing last night, around 3 o'clock before dawn, Somebody hacked into the security system of their house; getting inside and kidnapping Cole," explained Derick.

"Doesn't the Governor have securities around his house?" Danny asked.

I signed "Who would want to hurt a kid" looking at Cole's picture.

Danny standing from his chair "A sick person!."

"They're asking 1.5 million," Derick said in a devastated tone. "The governor asked for the best-case solvers, and that's you guys."

"US!" I stood up from my seat. "I haven't even solved Shelly's case yet."

"I will place someone else to solve that case, from all of the officers here in this building you have been the ones that have solved more than 100 cases," Derick said.

"How great is this," said Danny in a sarcastic way looking at me with a smile and then turning to Derick with a serious face. "I am not going to solve this case," said Danny walking to the door.

"Governor is willing to pay." Derick added.

Danny stopped, taking his hand off the doorknob. Looking to Detective Derick, "How much?."

"Half a million."

"I'm in then," rushing to his chair.

Derick looked at me, "will you, do it?."

"C'mon Eva," said Danny with a smirk.

"I'll do it if someone solves Shelly's case."

"Yes, I am going to put Max and Carmen to solve it," replied Derick.

"Okay," I said, looking at Danny.

Harry entered the police station. "Hey Carmen, where is my sister Eva," said Harry.

"She is in Detective Derick's office along with your brother Danny," replied Carmen.

"Are they in trouble?" asked Harry worried.

"I don't know, He just called them in a moment ago," she added.

Harry walked to Derick's office. Knocking on the door, Derick yelled "Who is it?."

"It's Harry." Danny opened the door. Harry can tell that Danny's eyes sparkled with excitement.

"What is going on?" asked Harry.

Derick's phone started ringing. "It's Walter! I need to tell him. And don't forget to tell Harry," he said to Danny and Eva, who were looking at Harry.

Hologram

Derick answered the phone while walking out of the room.

"Tell me what," said Harry, confused.

"Let's go to the bar to talk about it," said Danny. Harry sighed, tucking his shirt in.

Arriving at the bar. Harry sat in the middle barstool between Eva and Danny. Bobby the bartender came up to them.

"What would you guys like to drink."

"I would like a beer," said Danny.

"Me too," Harry said.

"Glass of red wine for me," I said.

"Be right back," Bobby said.

I breathed in "The governor son has gone missing last night; Derick says that the security system of the governor's house was hacked; kidnapping Cole and now they're asking for 1.5 million to bring him back home."

Bobby came bringing the drinks, "enjoy."

Harry sighed. "The governor can pay what they want, but it won't bring his son back. They'll just keep asking for more," he said, sipping his beer.

"The governor asked us to find his son. He checked our case record and liked what he saw. He's even offering us half a million dollars. Can you believe it?" Danny said as he finished his beer.

"Bobby bring me another beer!" said Danny.

"When do we start," asked Harry looking at me and Danny.

"Tomorrow, we start searching," I replied.

CHAPTER 2

I couldn't sleep last night. My mind was racing with thoughts of the suspects and who could have killed Shelly. Now, with the governor's son missing, I feel completely overwhelmed. Glancing at my clock upon my nightstand it was 2:39 am. Taking my sheets off, putting my slippers on. Trying not to make much noise so Danny and Harry don't wake up. I went to my desk, opened my laptop, looked through Shelly's pictures of family and close friends. I clicked on a video that Mrs. Cruz posted of her daughter in the park sliding down. I continued to scroll down there was a picture of her first tooth lost. Shelly was only 8 years old when she was murdered. Mrs. Cruz image was still in the back of my head like an unforgettable memory. She was heartbroken; she approached me on her knees, tears streaming down her face. The waterproof mascara didn't last from how much she cried.

"Your Eva right, you've solved a lot of cases, please bring my little girl back to me." The officers grabbed her, taking her away from me. "Bring my shelly back!" She yelled while they dragged her away.

My heart was shattered into pieces. I just stood there. Josh came to comfort me.

"Are you alright" taking my hand.

"Yeah," I whispered taking my hand out from his.

After that, I investigated day and night until I found Shelly's body thrown in the Black Lake on the seventh day. Police officers with their K9 and helicopters covered the lake. The police took her body out of the water. Placing her on the grass. I walked up to her to get a

closer look. I saw an innocent little girl with a whole life ahead of her. Shelly's skin was a deep purple color. She had an open wound on her right wrist. The paramedics came rushing, carrying her body on the cart, covering her with a white sheet. Mrs. Cruz came running screaming.

"NO!" grabbing her blond hair. "NO! my, my shelly stuttering on her words. Taking the sheet off from her daughter. Touching her purple face, hugging her.

Everyone was silent. Mrs. Cruz looked at me with tears running down her cheek then looked at her daughter,

"My baby, Find the bastard and kill him!." Mrs. Cruz cried out looking at me.

Josh knew that I felt overwhelmed and frustrated. I couldn't take it anymore the pain, I left the scene to find the killer.

I can hear Josh calling me "Eva wait!!." I didn't listen, I continued. Then suddenly Josh grabbed my arm, moving me aside.

"Eva, you have to calm down, you can't just go out there putting yourself in danger." "Whoever did this is dangerous," Josh said.

Dayeneliss Perez

He looked at me in the eye. I tried not to make eye contact with him because I didn't want him to see me crying. My eyes filled with tears, and I couldn't say anything, almost as if I had a knot in my throat.

"The FBI is working now on who did this, it's not your responsibility anymore," added Josh.

Danny and Harry arrived at the scene where they saw Eva with Josh and ran to check on her.

Danny said to Josh, "Shelly has been found." Josh nodded.

"Are you alright Eva," Harry said holding her. I looked up into my brother's eyes and began to cry.

"I'm sorry," I whispered. Harry hugged me tightly.

"None of this is your fault," added Harry looking at Danny. I can remember that day like it was yesterday. Suddenly, the light of Harry's room turned on. I closed my laptop and went back to bed to get rest for tomorrow.

CHAPTER 3

The alarm went off at 7:30 am. I turned it off, trying to go back to bed but Harry started knocking on my door, "Eva wake up!."

I got up from bed, went to the bathroom sink and let the water run, placing my hands together letting it full up with water and putting it on my face. Looking at myself in the mirror, grabbing the towel and patting my face with it. I went to my closet to grab a pair of jeans and a beautiful flowery blouse. Placed my hair in a high ponytail. I took a last look at myself in the mirror, taking a deep breath whispering to myself.

"Here we go."

Walking through the hallways I felt this tension in my heart. Harry was in the living room seating on the brown couch watching his phone.

"Where's Danny, did he leave to the station already?".

"Yeah, he left about 30 minutes ago on his motorcycle." Harry replied, placing his phone in his back pocket.

At the station Josh saw Danny at his desk reading files. Josh looked around the station, no sight of Eva.

"Where is Eva?" Josh asked. Danny looks up to him.

"Hello Josh, good morning."

"Oh, sorry Danny good morning, I just have a question where?."

Before Josh could finish his sentence Danny stopped him.

"What do you want with my sister," said Danny in an angry tone looking at Josh straight in the eye.

"Why I can't ask a simple question," replied Josh annoyed.

"Hey guys, what's wrong," I said to Danny and Josh.

"Nothing," replied Danny glancing at Josh.

Detective Derick came in a rush "come to my office quick."

Harry and Eva followed Derick. Josh was going to follow behind Eva, but Danny grabbed behind his shirt, pushing him away from Eva. Entering the office Danny shut the door on Josh's face.

"Danny please, open the door to Josh," said Detective Derick.

Danny walked to his seat leaving the door shut. Josh opened the door, upset by what Danny did to him. He took his seat across from Eva.

"Are you alright Josh," I asked.

"Yea, I'm fine," replied Josh, scooting his chair closer to the table.

"He's fine!" said Danny sarcastically smiling at him.

Josh was irritated by the foolishness of Danny. Danny and Josh stood up, both filled with rage. They yelled at each other until Danny punched Josh in the mouth. Josh was ready to punch him back but before he could do it, Derick held him back while Harry restrained Danny.

"Guys stop!" I yelled.

"He started it," Josh said.

"You deserved it and more," replied Danny.

Hologram

What Danny said caused Josh to get even angrier. As Harry pushed Danny out of the office everyone stood up from their seats watching Danny being held by Harry. Taking him out of the building.

"Let me go Harry!" yelled Danny.

"What the hell is your problem, Danny!" yelled Harry.

"I am so sorry for what my brother did to you, I don't know what has gotten into him," I said.

Josh touches his lip, his finger had blood.

"Your bleeding Josh!" I said.

"Yea, thanks to your brother for busting my lip," replied Josh.

I glanced down at the wood floor, then looked up at Derick. I opened the door to make my way to the station's main door, but Carmen cut in front of me before I could go.

"What happen?" asked Carmen.

I really didn't have time to explain to Carmen that Danny punched Josh, she's going to ask me why and I don't know how to reply to her because I don't even know myself.

"Nothing," I said.

Running to the door, I can hear her yelling,

"You know, Eva!" Carmen shouted.

I saw Danny and Harry arguing downstairs outside. Rushing downstairs to calm them both down.

"Danny! What has Josh done to you, you should have never punched him," shouted Harry.

"He deserved that punch and more," yelled Danny.

"You go inside that building and apologize to Josh," Harry said.

"I am NOT apologizing to that jerk who just wants to hook up with my sister." He left for the parking lot, got on his motorcycle, put on his black helmet, and drove off to the highway. I stood there speechless, looking at Harry as he said in a low tone, "he'll come back."

"Me and Josh are only friends, were nothing more trust me," I said nervously.

Harry chuckled, placing his hands in his pockets.

"You don't see the way he looks at you, maybe you see him as a friend, but he sees you more than that," added Harry.

I changed the subject quickly with Cole's case.

"Now what do we do," I said.

"Well, go back inside and continue on Cole's case and Danny can start whenever he comes back," replied Harry walking upstairs. Harry opened the door. As soon as we entered, Carmen was waiting for us at the front desk, walking towards us.

"Where's your brother Danny," asked Carmen.

Harry remained silent.

"None of your business." I said irritated.

Derick was behind Carmen signaling us to come.

"Rude!" replied Carmen as me and Harry were walking away from her. Harry walked beside me.

"She is so noisy, always trying to be in other people's business." Harry added.

Looking at Derick, I can tell he was pissed. Entering the office everyone was silent.

"Where is Danny," asked Derick looking at me and Harry.

"He left sir," replied Harry.

On that, Josh entered the office and took his seat without making any noise.

"Okay, now can we work," said Derick grabbing his remote of the projector. "These are the video tapes of Walter's house at the time Cole went missing."

Playing the video. A black van parked outside of the gate as the main gate opened gradually inward. The van door swung open. Three men in all black stepped out, wearing masks and carrying professional weapons. Entering inside the house. Two minutes later coming out with Cole. Covering him with a black bag. Dragging him to the van. Then the passenger door opened. A tall man also dressed in black, his black slick hair made him scarier, wearing dark sunglasses. Came out reaching the van door.

"Wait! Derick go back and zoom into the man's wrist, he has a bracelet with a chip attached," I said walking closer to the projector.

"Who has a chip attached to their bracelet," asked Derick touching his beard.

CHAPTER 4

"What do you want us to do with the kid," asked the man.

"Take him to the Lab," replied Mark facing to his screen with body diagram.

The man left for the room where he had locked Cole inside. The room was dark with cold drops falling from the ceiling. It was solid concrete. Cole sat in a corner, crying in terror. He can hear the keys jingling from the other side of the door and watching how the knob moves.

Taking the keys, unlocking the door. Terrified, Cole huddled in a corner, wrapping his little arms around his knees and crying. He can see the doorknob moving. Two 6-foot-tall men enter, grabbing Cole by his shirt, dragging him to the Lab. The place seemed like a regular house. Then they came to a stop at a wall covered with paintings by famous painters. Standing there for about 15 seconds the wall starts to open like a sliding door; white smoke coming out of the room.

"Place him to the seat," Mark commanded.

Cole began screaming, "NO! LET ME GO!"

The two men placed Cole upon the flat counter, holding him still. It automatically locks Cole's hands and legs with metal. Cole tried to escape, but it was impossible. The two men left the lab. Leaving him with Mark in the Lab. Cole began to sweat tremendously. The reflection in his eyes showed the terror he had.

"What are you going to do," said Cole breathing heavily.

"Just stay still, this would be quick," replied Mark putting his gloves on. Mark went on the right side of Cole with a machine in hand.

Suddenly the machine changed into a small blade. The machine had an attached robotic hand with a white glove. Mark took a needle from a grey steel tray beside him.

"Don't worry Cole, there is no need to be afraid, this will only hurt a little," said Mark focusing on the needle. Injecting Cole's right wrist, slowly putting the liquid in his body.

"NO!" yelled Cole. Slowly Cole began to feel drowsy. He could see Mark's mouth moving as if he was saying something, but his voice was slowly fading away. His eyes slowly shutting. Cole went to a complete deep sleep. Opening his laptop. Scanning everything from the chip he placed in Cole's wrist to his system. Waiting for the loading to be completed.

"Little more, c'mon," whisper Mark. "97, 98, 99… 100, Yes!." The chip scanned Cole's body forming his own hologram.

CHAPTER 5

Danny came to a stop at the Palm supermarket. Entering inside, walking straightly to the drink aisle. Opening the fridge door, grabbing a coke. Danny across from him saw a woman over 50 years old with black hair about 5 feet tall. She was trying to reach for a can on the top shelf. Danny saw that she was struggling. He walked to her reaching the can that she was trying to get.

"Here you go, ma'am," handing it to her.

"Oh, well, thank you sir," she smiled to Danny, "call me Becki please," added Becki, placing the can of corn on the shopping cart.

"You're welcome, Becki," replied Danny smiling, "have a good rest of your day."

Walking to the cashier, placing down the coke.

"Is that all it, Danny," said Lily the cashier.

"Yea," replied Danny. He took out his wallet from his back pocket. Taking out some cash. Handing the money to Lily. She pushed the register, placing the money in. Danny grabbed the coke from the top counter.

"Thanks Lily," said Danny with a slight smile. As he was leaving the supermarket. Becki came to the same cashier that Danny went to.

Putting down her groceries on the lane. Lily kept her eyes on Danny all the time till he left.

"Who is he?" asked Becki curious.

"That's Danny Valdez. He works in the sheriff's department. Him and his sister, and brother are considered the best in the whole city," replied Lily, scanning the groceries.

"He is very handsome don't you think," said Becki smiling.

"Yeah," whispered Lily. As she was leaving the supermarket Becki whispered to herself, "Danny Valdez."

Thomas, the private driver of Becki notices her coming to the car. He quickly rushes to help her out with the groceries.

"Thomas please load my groceries," said Becki opening the door of her Bentley Bentayga. She grabbed her laptop that was on the seat next to her. Turned her laptop on and began to research on the sheriff department website. Clicked on the search tab, typing Danny Valdez's name. A picture of Danny with a paragraph about himself appeared.

"Danny Valdez has been part of the FBI community for more than eight years; him and his brother Harry and sister Eva have solved more than 100 cases. They are considered the best-case solvers in the whole city."

Becki scrolled down and there was a picture of the three of them. Eva in the middle, Harry beside her on the left side and Danny on her right. The three of them had big joyful smiles. The photo was taken in front of the sheriff's department. Thomas entered the driver's seat. Accelerated the car heading to Becki's Mansion.

"Thomas by any chance do you know the Valdez family?" asked Becki. Thomas took a while to respond to Becki's question. He glanced at Becki from the rearview mirror, taking a deep breath.

"The Valdez family are you talking about Harry, Danny, and Eva Valdez.

"Yes, them," replied Becki looking at Thomas through the rearview mirror. He sighed, slowly pressing on the brakes on the yellow light, coming to a complete stop on the red light.

Thomas cleared his throat. "Well, I don't know much about them, but what I do know is that their parents abandoned them since little and their mom's sister Jenny has been the one that has raised them three, Years later when Jenny took custody of the kids. Their parents were found dead in their motel room from an overdose. I know Jenny personally; she is the most kindhearted person. She loves those kids more than her own life."

"They had a tough childhood," replied Becki looking outside her window, watching people walking in and out of stores with bags in their hands.

"But that didn't stop them from being the best-case solvers," said Thomas with a smile.

CHAPTER 6

"Well at least we have footage of the night Cole went missing," Josh said standing up from his chair.

Placing my hands on my waist, turning to the paused footage.

"Derick zoom out to see the license plate of the Cadillac," I said.

Derck grabbed the remote, zooming out. The black Cadillac didn't have a license plate.

"Damn it!" yelled Harry, hitting the table with his hand.

Unexpectedly, Carmen entered the office. "What's wrong?"

She glances at the projector, walking up to it, she asked "What's this footage?"

I looked straight to Derick to observe his reaction of Carmen bursting into his office.

"Go back to what you were doing Carmen," Derick commanded.

"I can help," replied Carmen.

"Not now," added Derick.

Harry watched Carmen as she was making her way out. Carmen slammed the door hard. When the door shuts. Harry looks at Derick.

"Don't you think it would be better to get as much help we can get."

"You're right Harry, but Carmen doesn't have enough experience to do something like this. I'm not saying she is irresponsible; Carmen does her job amazingly, but she is a rookie at solving cases and finding missing people; she's better on the front desk," replied Derick.

"Now we have to check on all the road cameras at the time the Cadillac was leaving out of the Governor's house, to see where it could've possibly gone to," I said.

Stepping out of the office and into the security camera system room, the first one that I saw was Toby in his chair with empty boxes of donuts and pizzas, also holding a big glass of chocolate milkshake in his hand. Toby survives out of junk food and desserts. No wonder he is overweight, then he complains about getting a new shirt size every month.

"What's up Eva," Toby said finishing his last bit of his chocolate milkshake.

"Toby, I need the road footage of two days ago near Governor Walter's house." I said leaning my arms on the countertop of Toby's desk.

"On it… wait why the Governors house?" leaning back his chair, crossing his arm curious.

"The Governors son has been kidnapped by some psycho."

"Really, who?" he asked.

"That's what we're trying to find out, can you please hurry Toby, and clean your mouth, it's dirty," I said, rushing out of the door laughing.

Toby quickly opened his desk drawer taking out a clean napkin, cleaning his mouth embarrassed. As I was walking towards Derick's office everyone was whispering to one another. I stared at everyone confused. Opening the door of Derick's office. Entering there was the Governor sitting at the end of the table covering his eyes with his hands. He seemed beat up, you can tell he hasn't gotten any sleep for the past days, his eyes were so red, and his right eye was continuously twitching. He was in great grief about his son missing. I felt this deep pain in my heart seeing him in those conditions. Walking up close to Derick to inform him about Toby.

"Toby is on it," I whispered.

Derck responded with a slight nod. There was a moment of complete silence for 5 minutes straight.

Until Walter began sobbing, "Why my son, why him; my wife is devastated, I am always trying to comfort her with a lie like our Cole is coming back home to us, and I don't really know," rubbing his two shaking hands together slowly.

"I promise you that your son is going to be in your arms again, He is going to come back home to his family where he belongs. I am going to use my entire strength and mind to help your family," I said.

Waltor looked up to me with tears running down his cheek, "really, you promise."

"Yes, I promise," I replied.

"Eva, can I speak with you in private," said Derick holding my shoulder taking me out of the office, walking to the kitchen.

"You can't promise that because we don't know if we are going to find him, we don't even know if he is still alive."

"Well, then we have to search harder, I am not going to make the same mistake," I replied rushing out of the kitchen returning back to the office. On my way to the office, Carmen came running to me.

"Eva can you please let me help you guys with this case." Closing her hands together begging me.

I sighed, "Next time this is a very important one and we have no time to loose, this is for your own safety Carmen."

Letting her hands hopelessly down, she sighed looking down at the wood floor. As I entered Toby was there handing a USB drive to Harry. That drive contained the security cameras of the road that night. On the left corner of the office, surprisingly Danny was there with his arms crossed.

"Shouldn't this be on the news," asked Toby.

Waltor was silent, he didn't respond to Toby.

"I don't know its Waltor's decision if he wants to do that," Josh said.

Waltor stood up from his seat, choking on his words, "They sent a letter to my mailbox saying, to not report this publicity or things would get worser."

"A handwritten letter?" asked Danny walking up to the table.

"Yes," replied Waltor trying to hold back his tears.

"Why a letter, were not in the 18th century to send letters to one another," added Danny with a sense of humor in his voice.

"Nobody writes and gives out letters," I added confused.

"He knows he would have been caught by a text message over phone, so he wrote a letter to not identify who he is," said Josh.

"What a smart little bastard," replied Danny irritated.

Waltor stood from his seat and headed out of the office, keeping his head down. Detective Derick was outside of the door when Walter opened it. He didn't even look at Derick or even say a word to him. Walter passed Derick and everyone in the building like they weren't even there. As Derick entered his office, he was surprised and upset with Danny's presence

"Well, well, well look who decided to make his grand appearance again," said Derick.

Danny took a deep breath and folded his arms across his chest.

"Here is the drive, y'all asked me; I am going to be at my office because I left a large pepperoni pizza, and I don't want to eat it cold," Toby said, barely being able to walk.

I glanced at the laptop sitting at the end of the table. Walking over, I brought it closer so everyone could see. Then I took a seat and powered it on. A password was required to log in.

"Derick what's the password?" I asked.

"It's my name," replied Derick typing on his cell phone. I typed his name "Derick" as he told me to do.

I clicked the Enter button, but a message flashed across the screen in bold red letters: "Incorrect password. Please enter the correct password."

Dayeneliss Perez

I looked up at Derick, who was deeply focused on his phone, typing rapidly.

"Derick it's incorrect," I said confused.

Derick didn't even hesitate to look at my direction or even reply to what I said to him. He was very concentrated on his phone, walking back and forth in the office. Danny realized that Derick didn't reply to Eva. So, to get his attention Danny made a loud shriek to get Derick back to earth and away from the phone.

Derick jumped, dropping the phone to the floor and held his hands to his ears tightly.

"WHAT THE HELL DANNY! Why did you scream like that," yelled Derick, irritated. Danny tried to hold back his laughter from Derick's reaction.

"You didn't listen to what Eva asked you, and being right now in Lala land is not the right time," said Danny rubbing his head. I glanced at Danny giving a thank you look. Danny returned with a smirk.

"Oh, sorry Eva, what was your question?" Derick asked.

"Umm, the password is incorrect," I replied turning the laptop to his direction, showing him the screen. Derick was quiet for a moment, staring at the screen. He rubbed his hand on the back of his neck.

"Oh, it's my name but spelled backwards, its kcired all lowercase."

"Good thinking," said Josh smiling with his busted lip.

"Here," Harry said, handling me the USB flash drive.

Hologram

I inserted the drive into the laptop. A small circle slowly going around repeatedly until everything began to appear. I quickly counted how many camera recordings there were, there were in total seven camera footages from the night of Cole's disappearance. Everyone was standing behind my seat, trying to catch a glimpse of the recordings. I scrolled to the first footage, skipping through 3 hours of the recording until there was sight of the black Cadillac without the license plate. It appears driving at high speed, making a right turn.

"Wait, what's the name of that road," asked Harry taking out a piece of blank paper from his back pocket, unfolding it. Zooming into the street name, "Silver Water." Then I clicked on the second footage, it showed them driving to a main highway. The third footage showed them driving straight on the highway. The fourth and fifth footage had no sight of them. So, I quickly went through the sixth footage, the Cadillac was getting off the highway taking a right on Frank Road. Eagerly clicking on the seventh footage, hoping to find more information. My heart beating twice as fast than usual. Everyone was near to watch the clip. This footage is one of the most important recordings because if this doesn't contain where they could've left too then we're taking one step back than forward. The vehicle didn't have a license plate making it harder for us to figure out the owner of the car. After two minutes watching the footage there was sight of them. The vehicle kept driving straight, suddenly the recording blacked out.

"WHAT!" I begin clicking on my keyboard. A pop came out on my screen saying, "No recordings available."

"Damn it!" rushing out to the door, going to the security system office again. Opening the door, slamming the door behind me loud, causing Toby to drop his water all over him.

"Geez, what's the matter with you, you're going to have to pay for a new door, I spilled all my water on me," Toby said grabbing napkins wiping his blue t-shirt.

"Sorry, Toby but there is a problem with the drive you handed to me earlier, quick question is that the only footage you have of that night?"

"Let me check, I believe those were the only footages." Logging into his computer. "Yes, look right here," clicking on footage eight. Toby began to look concerned. "How is this footage delated?" clicking on the ninth footage but they all said the same thing.

"We've been hacked," Toby said looking straight at me. Toby hastily typed Derick phone extension.

Now everything is getting even more complicated than it was already, who could have done this? The first person that came through my head was Micheal Mango. He knew how to hack into the banks system stealing people's money from their own bank account. He is also known for stealing the identities of people. Micheal was only 21 years old when he was behind bars for 5 years. He was released 4 years ago. Micheal is capable of this, I don't think on kidnapping Cole but getting paid to hack the security system to cover up the person that kidnapped, yes. As I was leaving the office, I came to a stop at my office. I saw Danny and Harry exiting from Derck's office, making their way to me. I opened the middle of my desk drawer, grabbing the key for the file locker room.

"Our security systems got hacked?" asked Harry worried.

"Yes, Harry all our security system has no recordings after the seventh footage." I replied

Danny responded with a big sigh, facing down to the wood floor.

Making my way to the end of the hallway, the last black door on the right side is the file room, where all the victims, suspects, and guilty people's documents were held at. Unlocking the door, the room was pitch black. I reached for the four-light switches on the right side. The lights began to turn on one by one. There were over 100 file cabinets in this room. Everything is in alphabetical order of the person's last name, making it easier for us to find who we're looking for. Going straightly to the file cabinet that contains the letter M. Scrolling through all those hundreds of files. After 15 minutes of searching, the file of Michael Mango appeared, taking it out and closing the file cabinet. I immediately open Micheal's file to find any house address, quickly glancing through his personal information on the bottom of the page there was an address;

"7501 Riverbend Rd,"

I heard the door opening and footsteps walking in my direction. I quickly closed the folder and looked up. It was Josh.

"Hey, I heard about the security cameras being hacked," Josh said approaching me, closing the distance between us.

Dayeneliss Perez

"Yes, they did, but I may have the person, who could've have possibly hacked it," I said swinging the folder.

"Okay, do you want me to take a look at that?" asked Josh.

"Yea, by any chance does Michael Mango still live in 7501 Riverbend Rd?" I asked.

"Umm," I believe so, but I can check his information," Josh replied.

"Yes, can you please do that because there's possibly a high chance that he was the one that hacked our security system," I said, handing him the file of Michael.

"I'll do that right now Eva." Josh replied with the look he always gives me that makes me have butterflies in my stomach.

Josh opened the door and reached out for the light switch, turning it off. He made his way to his desk. As I was walking towards Danny and Harry, I saw Derick in the far end frustrated with the whole situation.

"We might have a suspect." I mentioned.

"Who?" Danny responded, raising an eyebrow.

"Micheal Mango," I replied without hesitation.

Harry leaned his back against the wall, taking a deep breath.

Josh came to us with a paper in his hand.

"He lives in the same place, 7501 Riverbend Rd." handing me the paper. Detective Derick made his way to where we were, anxiously rubbing his forehead. Anybody can see how overwhelmed Derick was, causing everyone else to get nervous in the room.

Hologram

"We need to find whoever did this ASAP!" Derick commanded, looking at each of us in the eyes.

CHAPTER 7

I lean against the side, gazing out the passenger window. Millions of thoughts race through my mind. Impatiently waiting to arrive to Micheal's house.

"Are you alright?" asked Josh glancing at me with the steering wheel in his hand.

"Yes, I'm okay," I replied smiling to him.

"If only I knew what goes through that pretty little head of yours." Josh added.

"At your next stop make a left." GPS said.

Josh made a left turn; the road led to a beautiful pathway of oak trees surrounded by freshly cut green grass. Viewing the side view mirror, watching Danny and Harry in the back following us. After driving half a mile, a gorgeous white mansion appeared from a distance. Driving up to the roundabout, I noticed a lovely water fountain. It was surrounded by bright red and white roses.

You sure this is the correct address?" I asked Josh, unbuckling myself.

The GPS: "You have arrived at your destination 7501 Riverbend Rd."

"You guys sure this is the correct address?" asked Harry over the radio.

I grabbed the radio holding the button on the upper right to speak. Josh reached into the glove compartment and pulled out the folder. He opened it and checked the address. Josh handed me the file to show me the address, 7501 Riverbend Rd.

"Yes, Harry that's what the file says," I said.

Josh accelerated the car driving closer to the house entrance. Slowly pressing on the brakes coming to a complete stop. I got out of the car and took a deep breath of fresh air. Shutting the car door behind me, walking up the stairs. We were all facing the front door of the mansion. The double doors were a dark auburn color with two enormous handles. Danny stepped forward, lifting his hand to knock on the door. After a few minutes waiting, no answer, Danny knocked again but this time he knocked harder. In a few seconds, the door opened. An overweight short women dressed as housekeeper answered the door. Her eyes went straightly to Danny then at us one by one, glancing to the cop cars behind us.

She got herself on her knees and started to beg to us.

"Please, officers, don't take me! I can't go back. I have a family to care for," the woman sobbed, struggling to get the words out.

She appeared to be Mexican from her accent when she spoke English. Harry reached for her hand, gently helping her get up.

"Were not here to take you, we want to know if there is a Micheal Mango living here," Harry said bringing the women to her feet.

As she was getting up from the floor, I read her name tag, "Maria," I whispered to myself.

"Maria does Micheal Mango live here?" I asked her.

Dayeneliss Perez

"Yes, he does, he's my boss," Maria replied, rubbing her knees.

"Can you please tell him that we need to speak with him urgently," I said trying to take a glance inside the house.

"Yes, of course come in please," Maria replied, opening the door wide open for us to enter.

Inside the Mansion, the white marble tiles gleamed beautifully. They were so polished that you could see your own reflection. A gorgeous chandelier with crystals dangling off the tall ceilings. This mansion was so beautiful and luxurious that it takes your breath away.

After everyone entered, Maria closed the door.

"Please wait a minute here," Maria said making her way to a hallway.

I noticed Maria from afar as she stood in front of a door. She started adjusting her outfit and ran her fingers through her hair. Raising her right hand and began knocking on the door.

I overheard Danny and Harry talking quietly. They whispered about how beautiful everything looked.

Micheal was sitting on his lavish black leather chair smoking his cigar.

"Who is it?" asked Micheal rubbing his cigar against the ashtray near him.

"It's Maria," Maria replied.

"Come in," said Micheal.

Maria opened the door and entered the room.

"Guys, she entered," I said.

"Well, I guess we just have to wait until Micheal decides to make his grand entrance," replied Danny sarcastically.

"I am so sorry to bother you sir, but there are some officers waiting for you in the foyer," Maria said, nervously placing her hands behind her back.

There was smoke coming from the ashtray near Micheal. Sliding his chair back, taking a deep breath in as he was slowly standing up.

"Did you get their names?" asked Micheal.

"Umm, no sir," replied Maria stuttering on her words.

"Why did you even let them in my house without my permission Maria," Micheal said upset nodding his head as he was standing up. Looking at himself in the mirror to look presentable to meet them.

"Maria next time don't let anyone in my house without my permission again," Micheal said, as he was adjusting his white long sleeve shirt. Running his fingers through his hair and then fixing his dark blue tie. Micheal grabbed his suit that was hanging behind his chair. He was putting his suit on while he was making his way to the door. Maria rushed to open the door for him. Micheal held it open for Maria to come out first.

I saw the door opening. The first one that came out was Maria then a tall man behind her, he closed the door behind him. Making his way to us. He walked with confidence and dignity. I wondered if that was Micheal Mango. As he came to a stop to us, his eyes locked into mines. He didn't appear surprised by our visit; he was calm and respectful.

Dayeneliss Perez

"Good afternoon, officers is there seem to be a problem?" glancing at us one by one. "What a surprise to see you again Eva," Micheal added, sounding sincere about it.

I couldn't find the words to respond. Micheal has changed so much since I last saw him. That was when I began my job as a police officer. Now he is a completely changed man and quite handsome too. His dark green eyes were absolutely engaging, with his deep brown hair. It made it hard not to look at him. Josh realized that Eva's eyes were sparkling looking at Micheal. Josh cleared his throat.

"Michael, we came here to talk to you," Josh said, trying to sound professional despite his jealousy.

"Okay, about what exactly?" replied Micheal folding his hands. Maria quickly left Micheal's side and continued to dust the house.

"Can we please spare a few minutes of your time Micheal," I said.

"Sure, follow me," showing the way with his hand. Micheal went ahead of us to lead the way. As I was walking around the mansion. I glanced around left to right and up to down. Everything was so elegant and polish. The hallway smells like a garden of magnolia flowers. He made a stop at the same door he and Maria came out of. He opened the door. Entering inside the room that appeared to be his office. The office had leather sofas, and the desk was luxurious in the color black with its black leather chair. The office featured eight huge windows. They offered a stunning view of the landscape. The grass was so green that it even seemed unreal. Oak trees giving off shade. Micheal walked to his desk and sat in his black leather chair. Micheal reached his hand to his middle desk drawer. Josh rushed to grab his gun. Micheal saw Josh by the corner of his eye.

"Don't worry, I'm getting a cigar," said Micheal, showing his cigar to Josh. Placing it in his mouth and lighting it up with the lighter. He closed the drawer. Josh removes his hand away from the gun. Micheal exhaling the smoke out of his mouth.

"Please take a seat," Micheal said, He leaned back in his chair, relaxed. I sat on the leather sofa, resting my arm on its armrest. Harry sat beside me, in the middle of the sofa. Micheal's gaze turned to Josh and Danny.

"Are you guys just going to stand there?" Micheal said, continuing smoking his cigar.

"I rather stand, thank you though," replied Josh.

"I'm okay," replied Danny leaning his upper body on the sofas back where me and Harry were sitting.

"I may say you are beautiful today, Eva," said Micheal looking at me with a smile.

Josh drew a deep breath, placing his hands on his belt waist, bothered from what Micheal told Eva.

"Okay, let's get to the point here," said Danny.

"You guys tell me because you are the ones that came," added Micheal with a smirk.

"Someone has hacked the security system of the police station," added Harry.

CHAPTER 8

Cole was lying down, feeling lightheaded and struggling to stay awake. He slowly opened his eyes. At first, everything was blurry, but then he saw a flickering light above him. It grabbed his attention. He glanced around. The room was empty, except for a clock on the wall. Its rhythmic ticking broke the silence. Everything seemed so peaceful, there was no sight of Mark and the men's, his hands weren't tied up. Cole tried to get up, moving his right leg out and pushing his body to get out. Falling face first hard against the cold floor. Aching in pain, placing his two hands against the floor to push himself up but he couldn't, even though how much he tried he was too weak, slowly turning his body to face upward. Placing his small hands on his stomach. He hasn't eaten anything for 2 days, having a sharp stomach pain.

Suddenly, he hears the door opening and footsteps approaching him. Cole turned his head to face the shoes. It was a pair of glossy black boots. Cole slowly brought his eyes up to meet the person's face. It was Mark with the two men that dragged him. Cole tried again to get up to escape from them but nothing, he was way to weak.

"Take him away," exclaimed Mark to the men's.

In an instant the two men carried Cole, taking him back to the room where he was, dropping Cole on the floor. Shutting the metal door and leaving Cole in the ground. Cole can hear the man's voice fading away.

Moving his knees closer to him and began to sob. Remembering his family and how he wasn't scared, he was always sheltered, loved, and cared for. One of the men opened the door, throwing a tray that had a small piece of bread and a small bottle of water. Cole crawled, struggling to move with barely energy. As he was biting through the bread. There was something on his right wrist with three stitches perfectly stitched in. Cole was confused, not understanding what Mark had done to him.

The men that threw the food to Cole, walked to Mark's office to let him know he gave Cole the bread and water. Mark turned his head to face him.

"Good," said Mark.

The men's feared Mark because he would always threaten them by saying he'll hurt their families. The men knew what Mark was doing was wrong, but they still needed to follow orders.

"Get out," Mark said, turning his back to the men. He stared out at the pine trees through his large windows. Mark turned his head to the right, waiting for the man to leave his office. The man opened the door leaving Mark alone. As soon as Mark heard the door shutting. He carefully placed his hand in his right front pocket and pulled out a small remote. He held the remote with a hard grip, rubbing his thumb on the side. Walking back and forth in the office, hoping for his invention to work. This is Mark's first time he uses this remote to form Cole's body into a hologram, he has never tried this remote. Mark stopped walking and

Dayeneliss Perez

stood in the middle of the large windows. Staring at the blue button. He places his right thumb and begins rubbing the blue button in circular motion. Mark gave out a heavy sigh then pressed on the blue button. Suddenly, Cole felt this stinging coming from his right wrist. A loud pitching noise in his head began making him unable to concentrate. Cole placed both his hands on his head, trying to cover his ears from the loud noise. Then a blue light came out of nowhere from his right wrist spreading around his entire body. Trying to focus but everything was spinning in circles making Cole dizzy causing him to fall. When the light reached Cole's brain. His whole body went into a deep sleep. The blue light came out of the remote in Mark's hand, scanning up and down; Cole's complete body began to appear. After the hologram was completed the blue light from the remote disappeared. Mark was amazed that the remote worked. After years of hard work and dedication, everything he created finally paid off. Mark walked around Cole's hologram, amazed at how perfectly it resembled him. Everything looked perfect.

CHAPTER 9

Micheal sarcastically laughed at what Harry told him.

"So, you believe it's me, look I know my past isn't clean nor good to look back at but that's long gone," Micheal explained.

Micheal stood from his chair. "You are welcome to investigate."

I got up from the sofa and started walking around. Danny opened the drawer's opening folder by folder. Danny scrolled through the folders. He checked each file and glanced up at Michael.

"You're an investor?" asked Danny with curiosity, closing the file he was reading.

"Yes, I invest in many lands and have several businesses," replied Micheal.

"How exactly do you have all these businesses if your record isn't clean?" questioned Josh.

"I have my ways," responded Micheal with a grin.

No one could find any clue that might lead us to Cole's disappearance or to our system being hacked.

Harry walked up to me whispering over my shoulder. "Eva, I haven't found anything, I'm sure that Micheal isn't the one."

"Me neither there's nothing." I replied relieved but devastated because that still means we need to find the person. Micheal was resting in his sofa. Rubbing his lips with his fingertips staring at us thoughtfully.

"So, did you find anything?" asked Micheal annoyed that we were going through all his stuff.

"No," I replied. Micheal rise from the sofa, walking to his whiskey stand. Grabbing a fancy whiskey glass, pouring himself a drink.

"Would any of you guys like a drink?" Micheal asked raising his eyebrows, taking a sip of his whiskey.

"No, thanks," responded Josh.

"I would have drink, but I am working, maybe next time," replied Danny with a smirk.

"I'm good thanks though," said Harry.

"I'm sorry for the confusion Micheal," I said walking to the door. Micheal rushed to open the door for me. Before I left, he grabbed my hand, gazing straight to my eyes.

"If there's any way I can help on anything, I'm always here." Micheal said.

"That's amazing you can start by solving all my problems I have!" shouted Danny making his way out of the office.

I looked down, I hadn't realized that Micheal was still holding my hand. I pulled my hand away from his and left the room in a hurry.

"Eva wait!" shouted Josh speeding up his pace trying to catch up to me. I stopped, turning myself towards Josh.

"What happened back there with you and Micheal?" Josh asked, with a tone of jealousy in his voice.

"What do you mean?" I replied trying to cover up the fact that me and Micheal held hands.

Josh stayed silent and he didn't respond to me. Danny and Harry approached me and Josh. Making our way to the exit of the front door Maria came running. She ran like a penguin running to catch their food. I laughed softly looking at Maria. Tripping on her own feet.

"You guys are leaving already?" Maria asked.

"Yes, Maria we have to continue with our investigation," I replied.

"Oh... would any of you guys like something to drink?" she asked with a huge smile on her face.

"No, but thank you," everyone replied.

Maria opened the door wide open for us to head out. As I was making my way to the car the weight in my heart became heavier, making it hard to breathe. Opening the passenger door, sitting down, and placing my seatbelt. Josh open the driver's door. He didn't speak a word to me, how he would usually do. Turning on the car and accelerating leaving back to the Police Station. The driving was pleasant at least; the landscape views were stunning. I glanced at Josh driving.

"Are you upset with me?" I asked in a low voice.

Josh took a deep breath, "How can I ever be upset with you?" he replied, turning the steering wheel making a left. The police station appeared from a distance.

"I didn't like how Micheal was flirting with you," Josh added.

"That was nothing, I already told you," I replied to him.

"So, the way he was speaking to you and the way he held your hand that was nothing, seriously Eva," exclaimed Josh upset.

"He was just trying to be polite," I said looking out the window.

"Polite, please," Josh said mumbling under his breath.

Parking the car in the first available parking space there was. Josh parked the car and turned it off. He walked straight into the police station, not looking back. I unbuckled my seatbelt and opened the door, coming out of the car, closing the door. Harry parked close to our parking spot. Harry opened his door.

"What's up with Josh why did he leave immediately?" Harry asked walking closer to me. I looked up to Harry instead of saying that we argued in the car towards how Micheal was with me, I said.

"Nothing."

Harry placed his hands on my shoulder, lifting his both eyebrows up.

I looked up to meet his eyes and gave him a slight smile, "Don't worry about it."

CHAPTER 10

After sitting and thinking about Eva and the security cameras being hacked. Micheal was wondering to himself if he should help them or not. Then after an hour thinking about what he should do he decided to help them. Micheal ran out of his office rushing through the hallways. Maria was dusting the furniture. Micheal unlocks the front door and ran outside. Touching his pockets searching for his car keys.

"Damn it!" Rushing back into the house to his office, opening the top drawer of his desk. Grabbing his keys of his Porsche 911. As Micheal was hurrying, he came to a stop to Maria who was holding the front door.

"Maria, let everyone know I can't make it to the meeting today. If they ask why, say something important came up that I need to handle urgently."""

Rushing down the stairs, he pressed the unlock button on the keys, opened the car door, and started the engine. Stepping on the accelerator. He took off at 80 miles per hour. He held the steering wheel tightly with both hands and stared at the traffic light. He rubbed his hands hard on the wheel. The yellow light went on. He accelerated the car more.

"C'mon," whispering under his breath. Yellow light switching to red. Passing the red light in front of a cop on the left lane. The cop turned his sirens on, pressed on his gas petal catching up to Micheal.

Micheal glanced at his rearview mirror.

"Damn it!" hitting the steering wheel with his hands. Looking at his speedometer. He was going 90 in a 55-speed limit.

"Stop your vehicle!" said the cop through his mic. Micheal ignored it and kept on driving to the Police department. As he was driving, there appeared two more cop cars in both lanes. Making a sharp turn to his right, there were cop cars covering the road. Micheal quickly pressed his brakes so hard leaving skid mark on the road. Micheal glanced at his side-view mirror. He wanted to check for any cops in the left lane. But there were cops all around him. Micheal let out a devasted breath. He can hear the cops speaking through their mics.

"Get out of the vehicle now!"

Micheal reached to unbuckle himself, slowly opening the door.

"Place your hands behind your head and get on your knees!" yelled the cop approaching Micheal. He followed the cop's orders. Micheal stared to the sky kneeling; A helicopter was flying over him.

"Great," mumbling under his breath. The officer grabbed Micheal's hand in a rough way, cuffing him. The officer behind that was putting Micheal in cuffs pushed Micheal closer to him,

"Idiot!" the officer called Micheal, pushing him towards the cop car. There was another officer leaning on the car waiting to open the car door for him. Micheal took a quick glance at the name tag of the officer, "Ted." He was in his mid-40s, bald with a mustache, and blue crystal eyes. Ted's eyes looked at Micheal up and down. Ted unlocked the cuffs placing Micheal's hands together up front; cuffing him again.

"Think buddy before you race," opening the car door. The officer shoved Micheal in the backseat. Micheal quickly scooted himself to the middle with his hands cuffed on front of him. The officer slammed the door hard. Micheal looked at his cuffed hands and then outside of the right-side window. Staring at Ted and the officer that cuffed him. They were both talking to one another, taking quick glances at Micheal in the backseat. Micheal kept his eye on Ted as he was walking to the driver's seat. Entering the car, he got himself comfortable then buckled his seatbelt. Ted began to move the car. Micheal scooted to the right side of the seat, leaning his head on the window and let out a devasted sighed.

"So, your Micheal Mango," said Ted looking at Micheal through the rearview mirror.

"And you must be Ted," replied Micheal sarcastically looking back at Ted.

Ted's face was surprise that Micheal knew his name.

"Where are you taking me?" asked Micheal, sliding back to the middle.

"To the Police station," Ted replied, making a left turn.

"Yes!" exclaimed Micheal with excitement. Ted furrows his eyebrow, confused by the fact that Michael is excited to go to the police station.

Like who the hell gets excited to go to the Police station thought Ted. After thirty minutes of driving, they arrived. Ted pulled into the parking lot and stopped. Micheal looked out the window, waiting for Ted to open the door. Ted turned the car off, exiting the car walking to Micheal's door.

"C'mon," Ted said as he open the door grabbing Micheal by his arm, leading Micheal to the Police station. As Ted and Micheal were making their way to the Police Station there was Carmen at the front desk.

"Hey Ted, can I please speak to Eva," asked Micheal.

Ted ignored him and continued moving him.

"Ted please, I need to speak to her!" Micheal asked again.

Ted remain silent. Micheal yelled for Eva as he tried to run from Ted. Then, another officer stopped him from leaving. Moving his arms with his hands still cuffed, trying to take Ted and the other officer off him.

"I need to speak with Eva please!" Micheal yelled again.

Even how much Micheal begged to the officers to bring him to Eva they still wouldn't. Micheal got tired of them and stepped on Ted's right foot then hit his head against the officer face. Running to the front desk where Carmen saw everything that happened.

"Hi there, could you please tell Eva that I am here," said Micheal trying to catch his breath. Before Carmen could reply to Micheal, the officers got a hold of him, throwing Micheal against the floor. Taking him instantly to a room.

Hologram

The officer struck by Michael groaned in pain. He held his nose, which was dripping with blood.

"Uhm, he broke my nose," putting pressure on his bloody nose with blood drops on the floor.

"I'm going to kill that son of."

"Hey!" called out Ted holding his foot that was throbbing in pain.

Carmen quickly left the front desk to let Eva know about Micheal. She was in Derick's office, still investigating Cole's case. Carmen opened the door, making her way in.

"Eva someone is here wanting to speak with you."

"How many times do I have to tell you to knock before opening the door?" Derick said, upset and frustrated after repeating this to Carmen so many times.

"Who is it?" I asked, not having any energy to speak to anyone.

"Well, he is a very good-looking tall gentlemen, but he just got arrested, oh and also he hit Ted and Fred," added Carmen.

The first person I thought of was Michael. But it couldn't be him. We saw him just two hours ago, so he couldn't have gotten arrested.

"By any chance you know his name?" I asked.

"Nope," Carmen replied in a faint voice.

"I'll be there in a few minutes," I added taking a seat again.

"Okay," replied Carmen leaving out of the office.

Danny turned his chair to face me.

"Who is it?" asked Danny curiously folding his arms together.

Dayeneliss Perez

"I don't know," I replied confused.

CHAPTER 11

"Don't do anything stupid," Ted said, unlocking Micheal left hand and locking the chain to a hole of the table.

Micheal just stayed quiet without making a single noise and slowly sat down on the chair. As Ted was leaving the room he asked Fred.

"Why do you think he wants to speak with Eva?"

"I don't know, and I don't care," replied Fred.

Ted and Fred approached Josh's office where Josh was at his desk typing something onto his computer. Josh stopped typing and looked at Fred and Ted.

"WOW! What happened to you Fred," jumping off his chair in shock of Fred's nose.

"Long story, the guy that got arrested gave us a hard time," replied Ted.

"We need you in the interview room," said Fred holding his nose while talking.

"Okay," Josh left immediately, angry about what had happened to Fred. Josh burst the door open. Guess who he saw seating in the chair with his hands cuffed to the table, Micheal Mango.

"You?" Josh let out a deep sigh of disappointment. He placed his hands on his waist, resting them on his belt.

Micheal looked up to meet Josh's eyes,

"Josh, right?" asked Micheal.

"Yes," replied Josh, his tone serious.

Ted jumped in the conversion confuse that Micheal and Josh knew each other.

"You know this guy?" exclaimed Ted.

"Not really, we just met like 2 hours ago," added Josh.

"Can I please see Eva, I really need to speak with her," Micheal blurts out.

Josh drew a long breath laying his hands on the table.

"And why do you want to speak to her?" questioned Josh, frowning his eyebrows.

"I'm going to the bathroom to check my nose," Fred utters; while leaving the room with Ted who was also exiting the room, making his way to Carmen.

"Hey Carmen, where is Eva?" asked Ted.

"She's in Detective Derick's office," Carmen said, gently tapping the papers to align them.

"Okay, thanks," Ted replied limping on his right foot on his way to the office. Carmen sat back down in her seat.

"Why does everyone want to speak with Eva?" she whisper to herself.

"I can help her out," Micheal mentioned.

"Oh really, how exactly," questioned Josh.

"Can I just see her; I can help with finding who hacked your security system."

Josh remained silent for a good full minute, gazing thoughtfully at Micheal.

"Alright, I'll tell Eva you're here," Josh said, anxious about his decision. But if there's one person who knows hacking and computers, it's Michael.

Sitting on the chair with an unsolved case without any evidence to lead us. Am I capable of solving Cole's case, why me, why us, asking all these questions to myself.

Suddenly there was a knock at the door. Detective Derick walked to unlock the door. I looked up at the door to see who it was, and it was Ted; he rarely shows up at Derick's office. Derick opened the door wider for Ted to enter.

"I am sorry to interrupt, but there is a guy who wants to speak to you, Eva," remarked Ted, looking directly at me.

"Great," I whispered.

Josh burst into the office. He said Michael Mango is in the interview room and needs to talk to me right now.

"So that's the guy that has been wanting to speak with Eva," responded Danny leaning back to his seat.

"Micheal? What does he need to speak about and why is he in the interview room instead of waiting in the lobby?" I stated confused.

"Well, he actually got arrested," added Ted.

"What! Why?" I exclaimed, getting up from my chair.

Dayeneliss Perez

"He went over the speed limit, went through a red light, and tried to get away," Ted said, rubbing his bald head. I immediately left the office and left to the interview room where Micheal was being held at. Pushing the door open to encounter Micheal sitting on the chair like a punished child. I noticed the relief in his eyes when he saw me.

"It's so great to see you!" shouted Micheal.

"What have you gotten yourself into?" I replied with a smile.

"Let me explain myself: I have never engaged in speeding, except perhaps when I was a teenager, but that was many years ago. You can review my driver's license." I promise you," He explained standing up from his chair with his hand cuffed to the table.

"I believe you, but when you do speed you cause a catastrophe on the road." I mentioned with a soft laugh.

Micheal chuckled, returning me with a smile.

"Well, I'm out," said Ted limping out of the office.

Josh leaned his back on the wall and sighed staring down at the red oak wood floor. Harry knew Josh was upset; his face expressed everything. Taking a sip of his coke Harry asked, "Why did Micheal wanted to speak with Eva?"

Josh slowly brought his gaze to Harry.

"He said that he can help with finding who hacked our security system," Josh said.

"Perfect the more help the better," Danny added to the conversation.

"True but we shouldn't get help from him," exclaimed Josh angrily.

"Why not?" Danny responded, getting out of his seat.

"I don't trust him, there is something not right," mentioned Josh.

"Like what exactly? The man offered his help, yet you think he is bad. Remember, we showed up at his house unexpectedly and found nothing. Just tell the truth; you're jealous," said Danny, smirking as he waited to see Josh's reaction. Before Josh could respond to Danny, Derick interrupted them. He knew it wouldn't end well.

"Josh, Danny is right we need as much help that we can get to solve this case, if Micheal can help us on finding who hacked our system, he could probably be able to find who got into the governor's security system," Derick explained.

"Yeah," whispered Josh.

While I was in the room with Micheal. He raised his brown eyebrows, "Eva, I can help find the hacker," he said.

I sighed pulling the chair out across Micheal taking a seat.

"I appreciate that you are willing to help me but."

Before I could have said another word Micheal cut me off.

"I am going to help you whether you agree with it or not, and there is no way to change my mind," added Micheal.

Josh walked in and looked right at me with warmth in his eyes. But something felt off; he seemed upset or bothered.

"Eva, can I speak to you outside," Josh said.

I nodded following him out of the interview room. Josh was silent for the whole time, walking down the hallway. I rushed in front of him facing my body to his and met his eyes.

"What is that you wanted to tell me, you haven't said a word to me since we left the interview room?" I said.

He took me aside from the hallway taking some time to talk. It seemed like he didn't want to say what he was about to say.

"Umm… Detective Derick agrees on letting Micheal help us to find who hacked our system." Josh added fixing his eyes on me.

I was surprised that Derick would allow Micheal to help. Before I had a chance to speak Danny and Harry were making their way to me and Josh.

"Have you guys told Michael about the approval of helping us?" asked Danny, running his hand over his mouth.

"No not yet Josh just informed me about Derick's approval of it, we are on our way to let him know." I answered looking back at Josh, who was next to me.

As we were making our way back to the interview room, Josh held my hand pushing me against the wall. I can see from my side that Harry and Danny kept on walking their way to where Michael was at. Time seemed to go so slow looking up to Josh.

"Can I speak with you Eva please," Josh said giving my hand a gentle squeeze.

"Yes," I replied in a soft voice.

Josh led the way to his office, while holding my hand. He opened the door and as we were making our way in, I took my hand out of his. Closing the door behind us. I drew in a long breath. Josh began to walk towards me; I felt this weird feeling in my stomach like butterflies. I quickly turned my back on him.

"What is it that you want Josh?" I remarked.

Josh strolled around the room and then settled on the edge of his desk.

"Do you agree with letting Micheal help us? Josh responded, maintaining his gaze on me.

"I mean it's not a bad idea," I answered looking down.

Josh got off his desk and walked over to me, he came so close to me that I could smell the cologne on him. I kept my eyes on the floor, suddenly this weird feeling came to me that I couldn't say anything or move.

"Eva, look at me in the eyes," Josh murmured and with a tender touch, he raised my chin to look into his eyes. He wrapped his arms around my waist, drawing me closer and softly kissed me. My legs gave out beneath me. I broke the kiss and gently pushed him back.

"I have to go Josh," I said still having the sensation of his lips on mine. Darting out of the room with my feet still tingling from the kiss.

Josh looked distressed as I walked away. As I closed the door behind me, I rested my back against the door drawing in a deep breath trying to regain my composure.

Dayeneliss Perez

As I walked back to the room where Michael was, my heart was brimming with emotions. As I opened the door and stepped inside there was Micheal beaming with a wide grin.

"Are you okay?" asked Harry frowning his eyebrows.

"Yes," I replied, sliding the chair out and settling into the seat across from Michael. Josh quietly stepped in and leaned against the wall with his arms folded across his chest. Danny and Harry stood beside me.

"Did you consider my proposal?" asked Micheal making eye contact with all of us.

"Yes, we've agreed to let you help us," Danny said as he walked to the back of my chair and gripped the top of the seat.

"Perfect! "I thought you'd accept my offer to help. But after thinking it over, I need something in return," said Michael.

"I knew it," Josh mumbled under his breath.

"What do you want?" asked Harry.

"Well, to not take me to jail and to not place this in record," responded Micheal.

"Okay, we can do that. I won't place whatever occurred today on your record, but you have to find the hacker," I answered.

Michael stood up, stretching his right hand out to me.

"So, we have a deal." He added.

I got up and reached out and grasped his hand in a shake.

"Deal," I replied.

Josh approached Micheal, pulling out a set of keys from his back pocket and unlocking his left wrist.

"Thanks man," Michael remarked, rubbing his wrist. Josh responded with a gentle nod and then fixed his gaze on me. I didn't maintain eye contact with Josh. Micheal followed Harry and Danny as they were exiting the room. I rushed out of the room to avoid talking to Josh. On my way out, Carmen rushed over to me, grabbing my arm.

"Wasn't he arrested? Why did he come out uncuffed?" whispered Carmen confused.

"He is going to help us with the investigation," I replied trying to get away from Carmem. She tightened her grip on my arm, ensuring I couldn't leave.

"What's his name?" she asked.

"Micheal," I replied annoyed.

"Oh, so he would be helping with the case you guys are trying to solve?" added Carmen.

I got fed up with Carmen's endless questions. I removed my arm from her grip.

"I don't have time for all your questions Carmen can we talk later because right now is not the moment." I said, heading towards Derick's office to join the others.

Walking into the office, I spotted Michael with a laptop. He was so focused on the laptop that he didn't even notice me coming in. Harry, Danny, and Derick gathered around Michael. Josh was on the other side across looking at Micheal's screen. I approached to get a better look at what Michael was doing. Michael was typing and clicking quickly on the keyboard.

"Okay, I need the delated recordings and a USB, so I can transfer the recordings to it," Micheal noted.

Derick put the laptop that contained the recordings beside Michael's laptop. Harry searched through the desk drawer, looking for a USB. He checked the top two drawers but found nothing.

"Derick where do you have a USB?" asked Harry moving the objects around, searching. He opened the bottom drawer and there was a black USB with a red stripe in the middle.

"Harry, I don't know where there could be one check good," replied Derick keeping his eyes all time on Micheal. Harry grabbed the USB, closing the drawer.

"Never mind I found it," Harry answered, moving towards Michael and handing him the USB.

"Thanks, Harry," Michael said, plugging the USB into the laptop. He waited for the deleted recordings to be uploaded. Josh walked up to Micheal across the table.

"Whoever delated these footages must really know their technology very well," Josh said, looking directly at Micheal.

Michael stopped typing and directed his gaze towards Josh.

"Now you think I deleted all these footages? Look Josh, if I delated these footages, I wouldn't be helping you guys," Micheal replied, irritated.

Derick gave Josh a glance that meant, 'Stay silent.'

"Can I have a word with you outside Josh," Derick exclaimed, raising an eyebrow. Josh followed Derick out the door. Derick moved Josh aside, placing his hand on his waistline.

"Josh, right now is not the moment to argue, remember Michael is helping us," Derick said.

"Yes, I completely understand but there is something not right about this," Josh answered, nodding his head.

"You know what's really bothering you Josh... that Michael could be interested in Eva," Derick said.

Josh inhaled, tucking his hands into his front pockets. He didn't respond to Derick; he remained completely silent. Staring down at the floor for a moment. Derick left Josh and returned to the office.

I wondered about the conversation between Derick and Josh, especially since only Derick came back. I felt the urge to check on Josh, yet the thought of facing him right now was too overwhelming.

"Still waiting on the upload to finish?" asked Derick, closing the door behind him.

"Almost done," I replied in a soft voice. I observed the upload progress, eager for it to be done.

After a long wait watching the progress bar, the upload finally finished.

"Were in," whispered Micheal. "Next, I just need to access the background information," he said, typing rapidly on the keyboard. As Micheal was typing on the black screen green words began to appear on the screen. Everyone in the room were surprised with how fast Micheal was typing. This was the first time I saw how hackers do it. A whole long paragraph appeared with tiny letters. Micheal scrolled to the very last, then there appeared a 4-digit code.

"Hand me a piece of paper and pen," said Micheal.

Derick rushed to his desk, grabbing a piece of paper and a pen. Handing it to Micheal.

He began to write down the 4-digit numbers on paper.

"7812" Micheal's handwriting was neat and professional. He exited everything on the laptop, clicked the shutdown button, rolled back his chair, and stood up with the paper in his hand.

"These numbers could possibly be our savior on helping us in finding the bastard that did this," exclaimed Micheal with a smirk.

"Detective Derick, can you send someone to check these 4 digits?" Micheal asked, handing him the paper.

"Yes," responded Derick taking the paper out of Micheal's hand.

Derick looked over at me.

"Eva, can you please hand this to Toby," asked Derick folding the paper smaller, handing it to me.

"Yes," I murmured, hoping for this to give us a hint. Taking the note out of his hand heading out of the room. As I left the room, I noticed Josh standing against the wall. He noticed me looking at him. Returning with a warm smile. I smiled back at him and then walked directly to Toby's office.

I pushed the door open and made my way directly to Toby, who was sitting in his chair.

"Hey Toby, we need to investigate who owns the device that deleted the footage," I said, handing him the folded paper.

"Alright," he replied, munching on food, leaning his chair closer to reach the paper. Toby unfolded the paper and glanced at the numbers. Then, he started typing them on the keyboard.

"How did you find this number?" asked Toby, curiously.

"Micheal Mango offered to help us," I replied, impatiently waiting for Toby to finish.

"Oh, like the Micheal Mango that was arrested years ago?"

"Yes, that one," I said, grabbing a pen from Toby's desk. I clicked the top repeatedly as I paced back and forth. If Toby finds who owns the device, that is one step closer to finding Cole. Toby stared at me as I walked back and forth.

"Eva, can you please stop.. You're making me nervous. Watching you like that keeps me from concentrating," Toby said, glancing up from his computer. I paused and placed my hands on Toby's desk.

"Maybe the governor did something to this person and their taking revenge on his own son," I stated. Thoughts were going through my head.

Dayeneliss Perez

"Found it!" shouted Toby, "Jacob Smith."

"Jacob Smith," I mumbled under my breath.

"Yes, and it turns out that he is a Woodfield University student," Toby added.

"Well, let's get his location and ask him a few questions," I responded, heading towards the door to let the others know. I grabbed my phone and searched "Woodfield university." I visited the university's website. In big, bold black letters, it said, "Start your bright future here at Woodfield." As I scrolled down, it looked like a technical computer university. That's how Jacob knew how to hack into systems because he was educating himself into that field. I entered the address into the gps on my phone.

"Placing route to Woodfield university," said the GPS.

"You're going to Woodfield university?" questioned Carmen behind me, her focus on my phone.

Holding my phone from falling.

"Geez Carmen, you scared me," I said, slipping my phone into my back pocket.

"Yes, I am going to head there in a little bit," I added.

"Oh, why?" questioned Carmen.

"I'll tell you later, I have to go now," I replied, making my way to Dericks's office where everyone else was. As I opened the door everyone wore anxious and stressed faces. Everyone looked at me as I was making my way in, closing the door behind me.

"We found out who hacked the security system. It was a student from Woodfield University named Jacob Smith. Toby researched the 4 digit-number that Micheal found, and the owner of the device led to Jacob Smith," I said.

 A slight knock came from the door.

"It's Toby," shouted Toby.

Harry rushed and opened the door. Toby entered with a photograph in his right hand of Jacob then placed it on the table for everyone to look at it. A young guy in his early 20s had dark brown hair and hazel eyes. He wore black square-framed glasses. His eyebrows were bushy and dark brown. He had thin lips and a round nose. He didn't seem like the type of person to do any harm, but as my Aunt Jenny always said.

"Not everyone is who they appear to be. Always dig deeper to understand who a person truly is." Aunt Jenny's words would always come to mind whenever I look at a suspect.

"I did some background check towards him; he is 24 years old, and he has a computer science major.

"Eva told us that he goes to Woodfield university?" Danny said, gazing at the picture of Jacob.

"Yes, that was what his personal information said so he must be there," responded Toby.

"Well, what are we waiting for," exclaimed Josh eagerly ready to go.

"I'll get the cars prepared for us," called out Harry, rushing out of the room.

"I'll help Harry," added Danny, following behind Harry out of the door. The one that didn't even say a word was Micheal, he was completely silent towards the subject of Jacob Smith. It almost seemed like his mind was somewhere else, he didn't even realize that me and Josh were still in the room. Micheal was quiet off, he wasn't himself. It has been too much for him to tolerate in a day with all the police chasing and finding the 4-digit code from the device. I sensed someone watching me and saw Josh leaning against the wall with both hands in his front pocket. I felt this rush in my veins while locking eyes with him. I walked past him, but he unexpectedly grabbed my hand and pulled me closer to him. "Can we talk," Josh said in a low tone. My heart was racing with the touch of Josh's hand in mine.

"Not now" I answered softly, removing my hand out of his. I exited the room as quickly as I could. Michael sensed a spark between Josh and Eva. I hurried out of the building, pushing the main entrance door. A cool autumn breeze brushed my face as I went down the stairs slowly, stopping at the last step. I saw Harry and Danny approaching me.

"All done, tell the others that were ready to go," said Danny rubbing his hands together.

"Do you want me to tell the others?" Harry asked.

I looked directly into his eyes and nodded. Harry walked up the stairs making his way into the police station. Danny held my hand and wrapped it around his arm.

"Don't worry Eva were going to find Cole," Danny said, patting my hand with a big smile in his face making our way to the car. As Harry walked to Derick's office, he saw Michael and Josh leaving. Derick was behind them, locking the door with a pair of keys. Harry signaled with a wave for them to come. Josh spotted Harry from a distance.

"The cars are ready," remarked Josh, speeding up his pace on walking. Michael kept pace with Josh, and when Derick noticed, he quickened his steps to catch up. They all left out of the building, but Carmen got hold of Harry with all her questions. As Josh was making his way out, he began to search for Eva, but she was already in the car.

"Where are you all going? What are you going to do? Harry placed his hands gently on her hands, looking directly into her eyes.

"Look Carmen, I must go but I promise you that I'll tell you about everything," before pulling his hand away from hers, he gave it a soft squeeze. Carmen felt a tingle in her stomach from Harry's touch. She gave him a smile. Harry left outside, where everyone was waiting for him.

"C'mon Harry, we don't got all day," shouted Danny, out of the window of the driver's seat. Harry rushed down the stairs. He pulled the passenger door handle, got into the car, and took a seat.

"What took you so long Harry?" I asked, sliding into the middle of the backseat.

"You know Carmen and her questions," replied Harry reaching out to buckle his seatbelt. "Where are the others?" questioned Harry.

Dayeneliss Perez

"They went ahead of us, meanwhile we were waiting for you," responded Danny, driving out of the parking lot of the police station.

"And you know what's the funny thing," Danny said with a chuckle.

"What?" replied Harry, confused.

"That the university is 35 minutes away from us and Josh is in the same car with Micheal," Danny said bursting into laughter, hitting the steering wheel. I leaned back in my seat, looking into the rearview mirror and seeing Danny laughing.

"You know you're so stupid," I exclaimed, rolling my eyes and folding my arms.

"Why?" Danny asked, trying to contain his laughter.

I didn't respond to Danny and his foolish nonsense.

CHAPTER 12

There was complete silence in the car.

"You'll arrive at your destination in 22 minutes," GPS said.

Derick was the one driving with Josh in the passenger seat looking out to the window. Michael slid over to the left side of the backseat.

"Josh, right?" Micheal asked.

"Yes," Josh answered, resting his elbow on the passenger door, holding his head.

"How long have you been a cop?" questioned Micheal.

"7 years almost 8 years." Josh replied.

"Oh, and for how long have you known Eva and her brothers?" Micheal asked.

"I believe about six years," answered Josh.

"Umm," mumbled Micheal, "You and Eva are you two together?" asked Micheal stretching out his arms.

The gas tank began signaling fuel low. Derick pounded the steering wheel with both his hands.

"Damn it! we have to stop to fuel the tank up," Derick said.

"There is a near gas station on the right corner," replied Josh, pointing to the direction of the gas station. Derick put on his right blinker. Driving up to the gas station, Derick stops at a gas pump, turns off the car and exits out of the car. He pulled his wallet from his back pocket. Then he grabbed his credit card and inserted it. He typed in his 4-digit PIN and started fueling his tank.

"So, Josh," before Michael could say another word, Josh stopped him without hesitation.

"I'm done answering your questions," Josh said annoyed, rolling down his window to get air since the car was off. Observing the cars passing by on the road.

Michael knew that the only way to catch Josh's attention was by involving Eva.

"I was planning to take Eva out to dinner?" said Micheal, leaning back to his seat.

Josh looked over his shoulder to Michael, giving him his full attention now.

"Now I got your attention," Micheal replied.

Josh remain silent without saying a word.

"Oh, I'm sorry you two are a thing?" Micheal sarcastically said.

Josh remained silent for a few more seconds. He remembered the kiss in his office, longing to hold her again.

"No," mumbled Josh, "were not a thing." Though he wished he could say the complete opposite.

"Is that so? Because I saw the sparks between you two earlier. Eva gets nervous around you," Micheal added.

CHAPTER 13

"I'm leaving Jacob, I will be back in about half an hour," Luke shouted, exiting the dorm.

"Okay, see you then," replied Jacob typing onto his laptop, facing his screen, with a bunch of papers scattered everywhere on his desk. Jacob's bed was clean and tidy, but his desk was where he spends most of his time in. Jacob stood from his chair and walked to his drawer to grab his headphones. As he took his headphones and headed back to his desk to pair them with his laptop. There was a knock at the door.

"Really, Luke? You forgot your keys?" Jacob shouted, placing his headphones down near his laptop and heading to the door. Jacob opened it, only to find an unexpected visitor—Mark.

"Well, clearly, I'm not Luke," Mark said with a chuckle, stepping into Jacob's dorm and glancing around the room. "Anyone with you," asked Mark. Jacob's heart began to race with Mark's presence; he knew that Mark is capable of anything that is in his way and that he is an extremely dangerous man.

As he slowly closed the door, Jacob replied firmly, "No, my roommate just left," trying to hide his nervousness. "Do you need something Mark?" questioned Jacob, walking towards Mark.

Dayeneliss Perez

There was complete silence for a straight minute. Making Jacob more anxious.

Michael made a clicking sound with his tongue, turning his back to Jacob. "You know Jacob some cops are going to come here asking you questions about who send you to delete the footages."

Jacob was confused about what Mark was telling him.

"What do you mean? There's no way they can find us out," Jacob replied nervously, his palms beginning to sweat.

"Well, they did," Mark murmured quietly, slowly reaching for his handgun, which had a silencer. Mark quickly turned his body towards Jacob and fired, hitting him in the chest, causing him to fall to the ground. Jacob held his chest where the bullet had entered, curling up in pain and gasping for breath. Mark walked closer to where Jacob was lying on the floor aching in pain, He kicked Jacob to roll him over, and saw his shirt soaked in blood.

"Why did you do this to me?" Jacob choked out, struggling to catch his breath. Mark bent down closer to him. "There is no us."

Mark stretched his leg over Jacob's body and exited the room.

As Mark made his way down the staircase, he fixed his hair and clothes to avoid suspicion as he went down. His phone rang, and he pulled it from his front pocket, answering the call and bringing it to his right ear.

"Did you do it already?" a voice spoke through the phone.

"Yes, it's all done," Mark replied reaching to the end of the stairs, heading out of the building.

Hologram

"Hurry because they should be there any time now,"

"Don't worry, I know what I'm doing," Mark replied, pulling the door open and stepping outside. He drew the phone away from his ear and hung up the call.

CHAPTER 14

As we drove up to the university campus parking lot, I admired the beautiful architecture and the gorgeous landscape with oak trees. Students were sitting under the trees, while others walked around chatting with friends. Everything was well maintained. Danny parked at the nearest available space. Now, all that's left for us to do is to find Jacob Smith's dorm and interview him.

I looked behind to see if I could spot the others. "Where is Derick?" I asked.

"They should be here any minute," Harry said, unbuckling his seatbelt and opening the door. Danny turned the car off and exited. I moved to the right side of the back seat and opened the door.

"Should we wait for them," I asked closing my door.

"We should go and try to find Jacob and then they can come," Danny responded, looking at me over the car's roof.

"You're right," I replied, walking towards the entrance of the university. Harry and Danny were beside me. Harry grabbed the door handle and opened it for me and Danny. As we were making our way in, there was a young lady walking by us.

"Hey!" I spoke.

Hologram

She was incredibly attractive, early twenties, brown long straight silky hair, wearing a floral dress tight enough to show her hourglass figure. Carrying her notebooks and folders, wearing an earbud on her left ear.

"Hi," she replied in a dry tone, looking at us one by one, removing her earbud from her ear.

"I have a quick question, where is the front desk to find someone's dorm room?" I mention.

"Oh okay, yes continue straight then take a right turn then there would be a sign saying front desk, I don't think they would give you information of someone's dorm room though" she replied, trying to maintain her gaze on me and not on Danny. She kept on blushing when her eyes drifted in Danny's direction. Danny, as usual, knows when a woman is interested in him, so he smiles at her while looking her up and down.

"Okay, thank you for helping us," I replied.

"No problem anytime," she replied. As she was making her way to the door, Danny rushed to open it for her.

"Thank you," she said softly, meeting Danny's eyes as he held the door open for her.

"I'm Danny Valdez, by the way," Danny introduced himself, extending his hand.

"I'm Elizabeth," she responded, shaking his hand.

"Elizabeth," Danny mumbled under his breath, "what a beautiful name."

"Thank you," she replied, slowly pulling her hand back. "You should catch up to them." Elizabeth looked over at Eva and Harry as they walked off.

"Yes, of course," Danny responded rubbing the back of his head.

Elizabeth walked off leaving Danny completely enamored.

CHAPTER 15

"Guys hold up," cried out Danny running to me and Harry.

Stopping at the desk, but there was no one on site. A note that read, "Please ring the bell for assistance," with a little yellow bell beside it. I rang the bell twice, waiting for someone to appear.

"I would be right there," replied a voice.

Danny was over the moon, still smiling. I glanced at Harry, who was chuckling.

"Why are you smiling?" I asked.

"Nothing," Danny said, slipping his hands into his front pockets.

"What do you need dear?" A short elderly woman with grey hair above her shoulders looked over her glasses. The frames hung low on her nose, making her blue eyes stand out.

"Hello, I'm sorry to bother you. I'm Eva and these are my two brothers Harry and Danny, with the Police Department," pointing at each of them. "We're here for Jacob Smith. Could you tell us his dorm number?" I asked while staring into her blue eyes.

"Oh dear, what did he do?" she asked, nervously.

"We just need a couple of words with him," Harry added, folding his arms.

Dayeneliss Perez

"Okay, let me check," she said. She scooted her chair out and sat down. Then, she pushed her glasses up her nose and started typing on the keyboard. "Give me one moment, I am checking his dorm number." She grabbed a sticky note and pen and wrote down the dorm number.

"Okay, this is his dorm," she said placing the pen down standing up from her chair, handing the note to me. I took the note and read the number 545.

"Thank you," I replied. "Another quick question, where would this be at?"

"Go to the Lobby, then take a right. You'll find an elevator. Press the button for the 5th floor. After that, follow the signs for the dorm room numbers." She replied softly, "Anything else?"

"No, thank you again," I replied, heading towards the elevator.

Harry pressed the button and waited for it to open. The elevator beeped, and the doors slid open. We entered, and I pressed the button for the fifth floor. I watched the screen as the floors leveled by 1, 2, 3, 4, 5.

"Fifth floor," I announced as the doors opened.

As we left the elevator, we saw two signs. One pointed left for dorms 500-530, and the other pointed right for dorms 531-560.

"545," I whispered. "To the right," I remarked, heading in that direction. Scanning through the long hallway of dorm rooms and reading their numbers, I reached dorm 540.

"Were near," I said.

"545," it's this one," I said stopping at front of the door. The door was an oak brown color with golden numbers 545.

Harry knocked hard on the door; we waited but no answer. Harry knocked harder twice but still no answer.

"Open up the police department," shouted Danny banging on the door. I grabbed the doorknob. The door was unlocked. That surprised me. Who wouldn't lock their door? "I don't know where these college students have their heads at," I muttered to myself.

CHAPTER 16

Driving up to the university, Derick spotted Danny's car and parked nearby. Before Derick could completely park the car, Josh exited the vehicle and rushed into the building. Josh approached the front desk.

"Hey, how are you, by any chance did you see three people that came?" Josh asked, trying to catch his breath.

"Were they officers?" asked the elderly woman.

"Yes!" shouted Josh.

"They are on the fifth floor, they said that they needed to speak with Jacob," she replied.

"Okay, where is the elevator?" Josh interrupted her.

"You can't go to the dorm rooms," exclaimed the elderly woman.

"I am an officer too," remarked Josh, maintaining eye contact.

"It's at your right," she replied, signaling with her hand where the elevator was at.

Derick and Micheal caught up to Josh heading to the elevator. Josh quickly pressed the button. Impatiently waiting for the door to slide open. Entering the elevator in a hurry, he pressed the button for the fifth floor. Derick and Micheal rushed in the elevator to not stay outside.

"How did you know that they are at the fifth floor?" questioned Derick looking at Josh.

"They're on the fifth floor investigating Jacob," Josh said impatiently. Watching the elevator rise, then come to a stop. "Fifth floor."

CHAPTER 17

As I drew the door open, the first thing I saw was Jacob lying down in a puddle of his own blood.

"Damn it!" shouted Danny, grabbing his phone from his back pocket and calling 911.

I ran to him, holding his head and placing it on my knees. Jacob was as pale as a blank piece of paper, with no color on his face. He looked at me with pain and relief in his eyes. I gazed at his body to find where he had been wounded. His hands were on his chest. I gently removed them and saw the area where he was bleeding uncontrollably. Harry looked around the room for any cloth. He picked up the first T-shirt he found on the floor and gave it to me.

"Place pressure on his chest," Harry exclaimed. I grabbed the T-shirt and pressed it against his chest.

"He knew," Jacob whispered, barely being able to speak.

"Who knew?" I asked, hoping to get a name as I kept checking his pulse. His pulse gradually slowed down.

"Hang on, help is on the way," I told Jacob.

"We need an ambulance NOW! He has lost a lot of blood," I shouted.

I noticed Josh at the entrance, and he appeared to be in disbelief about what was happening.

"I did they are on their way." Danny replied.

"We have to take him down at the lobby," stated Josh.

"Yes," I remarked.

Josh and Danny rushed to carry Jacob. Danny got a hold under Jacob's arms and Josh held his legs, as if they were carrying a table. Derick and Micheal moved their way out of the door and faced me.

"Are you okay?" questioned Micheal, walking towards my direction.

I looked down at my clothes soaked with Jacob's blood. I have never seen this much blood in all my career years. It was a bloody mess in this room; whoever is behind this is capable of anything. My hands were shaking nonstop covered in dark red blood. I started to feel lightheaded; my vision blurred, and then I blacked out.

Michael rushed to Eva; aware she was about to faint. He caught her in his arms to keep her from hitting her head. He gently brushed the brown wavy strand of hair from her face.

"Will she be okay?" Michael asked, looking at Derick, who had his hand over his mouth. Then I looked at Eva. She seemed so fragile in his arms; unlike any other woman he had been with. He felt a connection with Eva being so close to him.

"Take her down," replied Derick.

"No, I think it's best for us to wait until she wakes up again." replied Micheal.

Derick walked around the room opening cabinet by cabinet searching for alcohol and a cotton ball for Eva to smell for her to wake up.

CHAPTER 18

Harry rushed down the stairs running after Danny and Josh as they exited the elevator, going to the lobby and rushing out of the building carrying Jacob leaving a trail of blood in the hallways and in the elevator, The sound of the ambulance was near.

"Let's place him down," said Danny exhausted from carrying Jacob.

They both slowly brought Jacob to the ground.

"He's losing a lot of blood he is going to need a blood transfusion," said Josh, holding Jacob's head on his knee.

"This guy cannot die!" exclaimed Danny, searching for the ambulance. As the ambulance appeared from a distance driving up, Danny began to wave his two hands in the air to get the paramedic's attention. The ambulance rushed in their direction. The ambulance came to a complete stop, and the two paramedics exited the vehicle. They both went to the back and opened it. They took out an emergency stretcher. Then, they approached Jacob, who was lying on Josh's knee.

"What happened," ask the man checking Jacob's pulse with his blue gloves on.

Harry and Danny both gave each other a quick look, the look they always give each other to see who speaks.

"He got shot in the chest and lost a ton of blood," Harry said, running his hand through his dark blonde hair.

The paramedics lifted Jacob onto the stretcher. Then, they quickly moved it into the ambulance. Danny rushed to one of the paramedics inside while the other took the driver's seat.

"What hospital would you take him?" asked Danny holding both back doors of the ambulance.

"To Waterfield Hospital," the paramedic replied, rushing to assist Jacob. Danny closed both doors and walked towards Harry, who was on the sidewalk.

In an instant they drove off. Josh looked down at his knees with blood stain on his pants.

"This is bad," Josh said over and over. "Whoever did this knew we were coming. Someone needs to warn them about us," he whispered.

"Who do you think it is?" Harry replied. The first person that came to Josh's mind was Micheal. He was the only one who could have warned the person behind all this. Josh stood up from the floor and walked back inside the university. He could feel his blood hot. Now he knew why Micheal wanted to help us so much to know what our next step was.

The pungent smell of alcohol reached my nostrils; I slowly began to feel my feet again and my fingers. My vision was still a bit blurry as I was opening my eyes. The more I blinked the clearer my vision began to appear. The person that I saw was Micheal, his green eyes had a sense of spark of joy when he saw me. Then I realized that I was in his arms, I quickly got up trying to maintain my balance.

"You blackout from all the blood," said Micheal, rubbing the back of his neck nervously. Josh entered the room, grabbed Michael, turned him to face him, and punched him in the mouth, causing Michael to fall to the ground.

I Immediately went to stop Josh before he beat Micheal up even more.

"Josh stop!" I cried out, holding him back.

"What the hell, Josh!" Michael exclaimed, noticing blood on his fingers after touching his lip.

"What's the matter with you!" Micheal called out, standing up.

"You Bastard! you warned the others that we were coming," replied Josh.

"Stop it!" Derick called out from behind.

"I didn't do that, and I also didn't warn no one about us coming here, I am capable of many things Josh, but not killing somebody," Micheal replied, spitting out blood from his mouth.

"Then how would they know that we would be here," Josh remarked. I was still trying to hold Josh away from Micheal before a disaster happens.

"I don't know, if I knew who is behind all this, I would take them down," responded Micheal irritated and constantly touching his lip.

"Please stop," I said softly, staring into Josh's eyes. Me and Josh locked our eyes for a moment and then he left the room in an instance, Derick followed him outside angry.

"I think he broke my lip," Micheal said as he walked to the bathroom. He turned on the light and looked at himself in the mirror.

"He did break my lip," Micheal said leaning down to the sink. Turning the water on and placing it at a warm temperature, waiting for the water to get warmer. He looked at himself in the mirror and saw me behind walking up to him.

"I'm sorry for the way Josh acted, he has never done something like that before," I said, while walking closer to Micheal who was washing his mouth. Micheal came to a stop and took the bottom of his white shirt and wiped his mouth.

"I don't need you to apologize to me, I need an apology from him, he had no reason to punch me like that," Micheal responded, slowly approaching me. I started to step back till my back was against the bathroom wall.

"He is afraid of losing you, I would too if I were him," Micheal closing the space between us, brushing a strand of my hair back behind my ear. Trying to not show Micheal on how nervous I was with him; I couldn't dare to see him in the eyes.

"I have to go," I whispered. Trying to leave but Micheal placed his hand on the wall, making sure I don't leave.

"Do you love him?" questioned Micheal, drawing his hand under my chin to meet his eyes.

"Who?" I replied, knowing that the person he meant was Josh.

"You know exactly who I am talking about," Micheal answered in a faint voice with his pupils dilated.

"Why are you asking me this?" I added gazing at his broken lip.

"I just want to know," Micheal responded, "I can tell that he feels something towards you."

I can feel the back of my ears getting hot, I had no words to reply to Micheal, I slightly pushed him away, exiting the bathroom and leaving the dorm.

CHAPTER 19

Entering the elevator, pressing the Lobby button. The door slid shut. Looking down at my clothes stained with Jacob's blood. The last words of Jacobs were roaming through my mind like a repetitive recording,

"He knew," for sure it was a man because he said "he" if it was a woman, he would have said "she" but who could have done this. I must go to the hospital and figure out who is behind this. The elevator opened. I stepped out and headed to the lobby. Pushing the door open. I saw Harry and Danny who were both leaning on the car talking to one another. I looked at Derick who was on the phone speaking low, but I can tell by his facial expression that it wasn't anything good.

"Are you upset with me?" Micheal whispered behind me. I jumped, turning quickly to him.

"You scared me. "No, of course I'm not upset with you," I replied as I looked directly into his eyes.

"You know, Eva, there's something about you that captivates me," Michael added.

"Really, what exactly," I replied, raising an eyebrow.

Before Michael could say a word, Josh interrupted,

"We have to leave, Michael."

Dayeneliss Perez

Micheal let out a devasted breath, "okay Josh," grinning, while walking to Josh's direction. Derick rushed to the car, opening the passenger door. "Josh you are going to drive," seating down and shutting the door.

"Yes sir," replied Josh grabbing the handle of the car door. Micheal opens the back door entering inside. Josh started the car and shifted into reverse. He backed out of the university parking lot and headed toward the police station. I walked up to Danny and Harry who were still having their conversation. As I walked towards them, they both stopped talking and turned to face me, both with wide smiles on their faces.

"Let's go home I need to take a shower," I said looking at my clothes.

"Yeah, you do," Harry said with a chuckle. He opened the back door for me. I smiled at him as I got into the car. Harry shut the door and walked around the car opening the passenger door. Danny was in the driver's seat. As we were on our way home Danny was completely silent, he hadn't said a word since we left the university. Which is strange because Danny is the most talkative one among the three of us. Harry gave me his side eye look then looked at Danny.

"What's wrong Danny," I asked moving myself forward. Danny looked at me from the corner of his eye.

"Whoever is behind this knows what we are going to do next, Eva after you're done taking a shower, we have to go to the hospital," responded Danny driving up to the driveway of our house.

"Yes, I am going to make it quick," I replied hoping out of the car.

CHAPTER 20

Nothing is better than a warm shower. I feel such a relief afterwards. Making my way out of the shower, I saw my clothes on the floor with Jacob's blood stained onto them. I dried my body with a towel and placed my clothes on. The mirror of the bathroom was foggy. I grabbed a small towel and wiped the fog away to see my reflection. I opened the top bathroom sink drawer, took my hairbrush, and softly combed my hair. After I finished brushing my hair, I took a moment and looked at myself and took a deep breath. So many things have happened all at once, it's so frustrating. I left the bathroom and went to my room. Grabbing my pair of shoes that were near my closet door. Sitting on the corner of my bed putting on my socks first then my shoes. I walked up to my mirror to check myself one last time and went out of my room. As I was making my way downstairs, Danny and Harry were in the kitchen. Danny was taking his last bite on his apple and Harry was sipping on a water bottle.

"Okay, I'm ready, we can go now to the hospital," I mentioned, moving my hair to the side.

"Perfect let's go," replied Danny, rushing out to the door. Harry came up to me with an apple in his hand.

"Here in case, you're hungry because you haven't eaten anything," said Harry in a low voice handing me the apple.

"Thank you," I replied with a smile, taking the apple. We both followed Danny outside the house. Harry locked the front door with the keys. Danny entered the driver's seat, turning the car on. I hoped in the backseat and Harry went to the passenger seat. Danny placed the car on reverse driving out of the driveway. My phone began to ring. I took it out from my back pocket, it was Josh. I answered the call and placed the phone to my ear.

"Are you guys coming to the hospital?" asked Josh.

"Yes, we are actually on our way now, why?" I replied.

"Oh okay, just wanted to know because we have arrived at the hospital already," added Josh.

"Well, see you there then," I replied, ending the call.

When I ended the call with Josh, Harry looked over his shoulder.

"Who called?" he asked, curious.

"Josh," I replied.

After a straight 15 minutes of complete silence. Danny exhaled loudly.

"What's wrong Danny?" I asked worried.

"Everything is wrong," Danny responded.

I remained silent.

Driving up to the hospital, Danny parked into the parking lot close to the entrance of the hospital. We all exited the car and rushed inside the hospital. The door automatically slides open when we approached the entrance. Harry walked ahead of us to the receptionist. The women was in her late 20s with her nurse scrub uniform. She had beautiful crystal blue eyes and a bright smile. It took a moment for Harry to speak, I guess he got caught up with the nurse's beauty.

"Umm, hi," said Harry leaning onto the counter.

"Hi, can I help you with something?" she replied with a vibrant smile.

"Yes, were here for Jacob Smith, he was brought earlier in an ambulance from a gunshot wound," added Harry, trying to maintain his focus.

"Yes, I attended him when they brought him in, you guys are family?" asked the nurse looking at each one of us.

"No, we're officers, we are handling his case right now," responded Harry with a grin.

"Okay, just sign this paper, and I'll take you to his room," the nurse said, giving Harry a clipboard with a sign-in sheet and a pen attached.

Harry signed his name and handed it to Danny who was beside him. Danny signed his name and handed it to me, then I handed it back to the nurse.

"Thank you, follow me," she said getting out of her desk. Walking towards the door, she scans her ID for the door to unlock. We followed her in. While I walked through the hospital hallways, I saw a patient in each room. A few nurses were pushing patients in wheelchairs. Doctors are in a rush, stressed over the hospital work.

"I'm Harry," mentioned Harry to the nurse. She turned her face to Harry's direction.

"I'm Olivia," she replied with a smile.

"You're very beautiful, I mean your name is very beautiful, not that I mean that you're not beautiful, you are very beautiful," Harry said stuttering on his words. Olivia blushed, her cheeks were rosy, pink. She came to a stop; Olivia knocked lightly on the door. Softly opening the door.

"I'm coming in," she said in a low voice as she was opening the door.

We all went into the room. Jacob was on the hospital bed with a blood transfusion bag connected to his vein. There was a woman in her mid-50s and a young woman that seemed familiar to me, but who is it, I quite can't remember.

"There are some visitors here to see Jacob," said Olivia, checking all the monitors to see how Jacob was.

"You guys again?" said Elizabeth, surprised.

"Danny!" exclaimed Becki.

"Mom, you know this guy?" asked Elizabeth, looking at Becki and Danny confused.

"Wait that's your mom," added Danny in shock, pointing at Becki.

"Yes," she replied, gazing at Danny's eyes.

"I'm so glad to see you," added Becki placing her hand on Danny's shoulder.

Elizabeth broke eye contact with Danny. He didn't want to break eye contact, but then he turned to face Becki, who stood in front of him with red, swollen eyes from all the crying. Danny's eyes continuously drawn to Elizabeth, who was standing beside Jacob's bed. Elizabeth can feel Danny's eyes on her, but she didn't dare to look back into his eyes.

Becki noticed that Danny's eyes were on Elizabeth.

"This is my daughter Elizabeth," mentioned Becki, holding Danny's arm, walking him up to Elizabeth.

"Yes, we've met before in the university earlier today," responded Elizabeth softly, looking up at Danny.

"Oh, so you know each other already, how perfect," said Becki with a smile.

"No, not that well, we just encountered each other earlier today," added Elizabeth placing her hands behind her back.

"I would love to get to know you," Danny's gaze lit up with a vibrant spark as he looked at Elizabeth. She softly blushed, turning her eyes away to escape his. Meanwhile, Becki turned her focus toward Harry and me.

"And you must be Eva and Harry," Becki said walking to us.

"Yes," me and Harry replied confused on how this woman knew our name and how she knew Danny.

I looked over at Danny. He was baffled, shrugging his shoulders, not knowing what had just happened.

"I'm sorry, I'm Becki, Jacob's aunt," she said.

"Oh okay," I replied, I can tell that this woman is completely hurting, the reflection of her eyes showed it.

"I'll be back," remarked Olivia, making her way to the door. Harry rushed to the door to open it for her.

"Thank you, Harry" she said smiling as she was exiting the room.

"She remembered my name," whispered Harry to himself.

"Why are you guys here?" asked Elizabeth.

"We're here because we're solving Jacob's case. We found him in his dorm," Danny said, putting his hands in his pockets.

"So, your detectives?" questioned Elizabeth.

"No honey, there officers and one of the best," exclaimed Becki.

"Were a little bit of everything but yes we are officers," I responded, "Were here to ask you some questions." I added looking at Becki and Elizabeth.

Danny pulled a chair out for Elizabeth and Becki, to sit down while answering the questions.

They were both quiet when they sat down on their seats.

I cleared my throat to begin asking all the questions.

"Okay, so you are the aunt of Jacob," I mentioned looking at Becki that had her hands folded together.

"Yes, I am," she replied, quietly.

"And you must be his cousin," I added, looking at Elizabeth, who was deeply engaged in listening to me.

"Yes," she replied, "were particularly siblings," she added.

"What has Jacob been up to lately, have you notice any different or weird behavior from him?" I asked.

"I mean we would always talk over the phone but lately like 3 months ago he hasn't really been in communication with me," replied Becki, "which is weird because we would always talk."

Harry was recording all their answers in his phone to have it for record.

"What about you, Elizabeth," I asked.

"I haven't really been in communication with him, we would cross each other on the hallways but he never really wanted to hang out, or tell me anything, he would always push me aside," she responded softly.

"Okay," I said.

"Would any of you perhaps know who would want to hurt Jacob?" questioned Danny leaning against the wall with his arms folded.

"There is one guy that could possibly want to hurt Jacob," mentioned Becki.

Danny breathed in deeply, slowly approaching them both.

"Who?" asked Danny.

"Bryce," said Becki.

"Wait, What! No mom he is not capable to hurt Jacob this way!" exclaimed Elizabeth, standing up from her seat.

"Who's Bryce?" I asked.

"He is Elizabeth's ex-boyfriend, he and Jacob got into a fight once because Jacob found out what Bryce did to Elizabeth, Bryce called out to Jacob that he will get paid for what he did. I think he could have been the one," remarked Becki.

"No, he wouldn't," Elizabeth exclaimed, continuously nodding her head.

"Anyone else?" I asked.

"No, Bryce is the only one in top of my head," replied Becki, firmly.

"What did he do to you," asked Danny, deeply concerned.

"It's none of your business," Elizabeth responded quietly, "Look I don't know who could possibly have done this to my cousin, but I know it wasn't Bryce because he is a coward, he would never be capable of doing this," Elizabeth explained, rushing out of the room. Danny rushed out following her exiting out of the hospital.

"Maybe I am wrong and it's someone else that could have done this to Jacob," added Becki regretting about what she had said of Bryce, knowing how much it hurt Elizabeth mentioning the name of that man. The gust of wind blew through Elizabeth's long, silky brown hair.

"Elizabeth wait!" yelled Danny running after her. Grabbing her arm, pulling her closer to him. There was a tear rolling down Elizabeth's cheek. She met Danny's eyes.

"I don't want to see him, Danny," she whispered. Danny pulled her in, wrapping his hands around her to give her a hug.

"Okay, but let's go inside because its cold," whispered Danny close to her ear.

Olivia rushed into the room concerned by Elizabeth rushing out and Danny behind her.

"What happened?" she asked.

"Nothing don't worry about it," replied Harry walking to Olivia. The door slightly open it was Josh and Micheal.

"You're here, great," I said, delighted from their presences. Both Josh and Micheal smiled.

"We've been here, we were just in the cafeteria waiting for you guys, until Olivia said that you guys were here," said Micheal, with a smirk.

CHAPTER 21

I stayed in the hospital room alone with Becki while the others were in the waiting room. There was complete silence for a few minutes. Becki was sitting on a nearby chair by Jacob. Wiping her tears with the tissue paper soaked with her tears. I quickly glanced around the room for a tissue box. There was one on a small desk in the corner of the room. I walked up to it and took a few tissues, slowly walking up to Becki sobbing.

"Here," I said in a low voice. She looked at me with tears rolling down her cheeks, with a slight smile. She gently took the tissues from my hand. Then, she wiped her eyes and blew her nose. It was stuffy from all the crying.

"Thank you, Eva," Becki quietly said. I was in shock that this woman knew my name from where? Becki realized that I was still confused.

"I met your brother once at a supermarket," Becki added rolling the tissue paper into a ball.

"Oh, I was wondering how you knew," I said with a sigh of relief.

Becki faced again to Jacob lying in a coma. Her eyes began to tear up again.

"I promise my sister that I will take good care of Jacob," Becki added, choking up with her words. "I've failed. Look at him! Her only child is in this condition. This is all my fault," Becki cried, resting her face against Jacob's arm.

"This is not your fault; we don't know why things like this happen, but they do, and you have to stay strong when it does." I mention, trying to comfort her somehow.

"Did you know anyone that would possibly want to hurt Jacob?" I questioned again, walking across the hospital bed, facing her. Becki looked at me with glassy eyes. Memories came back from Mrs. Cruz, Shelly's mother when she looked at me, begging me to find the murder of her daughter, that memory would always stay with me no matter how much I try to erase it, everything comes back to Shelly's case. I really hope Carmen and Max are working on Shelly's case.

"Jacob never had many friends. He would be alone most of the time, I don't know who would do this to him, he is a good kid," Becki added, brushing her hand over Jacob's hair, giving him a small kiss on his forehead. I took a deep breath, trying to almost swallow my emotions and be strong. Becki never knew about Jacob hacking our system, he probably never mentioned that to her nor to his cousin Elizabeth.

"What is one person he would be with daily? I asked myself. A sudden knock appeared at the door. Becki looked up in the direction of the door.

"Who is it?" I called out.

"May I come in please, its Luke, the roommate of Jacob." Luke said anxiously. I walked up to the door and opened it. Luke entered rushing to Jacob.

Dayeneliss Perez

"What happened?" Luke asked in shock looking at the condition Jacob was in.

"I should have stayed in the dorm. I could have stopped this. I warned him," Luke whispered, facing Jacob and Becki. The words repeated in my head. What did he mean by warning him?

"What do you mean by that," I said, staring directly into his eyes. Luke began to appear nervous; he didn't want to answer my question. He was changing the conversation by talking to Becki.

"Luke what did you mean by that, do you know who could have done this?" I questioned him again, walking closer to him. Luke remains silent, unable to maintain eye contact with me.

"SPEAK Luke!" Becki called out, desperately for an answer.

"Do you truly care for Jacob?" I asked him.

"Of course, I do he's like a brother to me," he replied, looking at me then at Jacob on the coma.

"If you tell me who did this, you'll help find justice for Jacob and for that person to not harm anyone else," I said.

"I don't know who he is, but there was a man who came to our dorm several times. He pressured Jacob to do favors or else he'd face serious trouble. I told Jacob to report him to the police because that man was trouble. But Jacob said to keep quiet and not tell anyone. Now look at what happened," Luke said, sounding regretful for not warning anyone.

"This is all my fault," Luke mumbled under his breath.

I placed my hand on his shoulder; he faced his eyes on mine.

"Don't blame yourself, it's not your fault," I added.

"His name is Mark," Luke said, looking at me and Becki.

"Why didn't you at least tell me," Becki said, crying.

"I'm sorry," responded Luke, deeply feeling regretful.

"I am going to leave you both, I have to do something now," I said, rushing out of the hospital room. As I was making my way-out Josh was leaning on the wall next to the door.

"Where are you going?" He asked.

"I have to go to the police station," I replied, walking out of the hospital. "I'll drive you there," Josh offered, catching up to my pace. "Eva wait," Josh said, grabbing my arm and pulling me close to him.

"What is it Josh, I can't loose time, this man is out there somewhere hurting innocent life's," I responded maintaining eye contact with Josh. "You found out who did this to Jacob?" asked Josh, still holding my arm.

"Yes, the roommate of Jacob, Luke told me that it's a man that would force Jacob to do things for him, his name is." I replied, anxious, before I could have said his name, Micheal showed up.

"Why are you two out here alone?" Micheal called from afar as he walked toward us. Josh slowly let's go of my arm. It's colder than I expected. The temperature is dropping, and I left my sweater at the police station on my chair. I had goosebumps. Josh noticed that I was cold. He removed his jacket and handed it to me.

"I'm fine, Josh don't worry, that's your jacket," I said, pushing the jacket back to him. Josh swung his jacket around me and pulled me closer. My heart skipped a beat.

"What about you, you're going to get cold," I said softly, as I was slowly getting lost in his eyes. Whenever I'm with Josh he feels like my safe heaven, I can't think straight, my stomach gets butterflies.

"Don't worry, I'll be fine. I'm wearing a long sleeve shirt," He replied, brushing his hand through my hair and placing it behind my ear. We were both lost with one another that we forgot that Micheal was there. Micheal cleared his throat loudly to make his presence known. I took a step back to make space between me and Josh.

"Did I interrupt something?" Micheal sarcastically spoke.

"No," I quickly answered, "we were just on our way to the station," I said, gently putting the jacket on.

"Hmm… okay," replied Micheal with a sound of doubt in his voice.

CHAPTER 22

As we were making our way into the station, everything was quiet, all you can hear are some whispers from a few people. Walking to Derick's office. Josh knocked on the door and Derick called out from inside.

"Who is it?"

"It's Josh, Eva and Micheal are with me," replied Josh. Then Derick unlocked the door and opened it. My phone began to ring from my back pocket. I took it out, it was Danny.

"I have to take this," I called out, showing the phone ringing. Answer the call and placed it to my ear.

As I was walking to a corner to speak to Danny, Josh and Micheal entered to Derick's office.

"Where are you Eva," asked Danny, sounding worried over the phone.

"I came to the police station; Luke told me the name of the guy." I said walking towards my office.

"Yea, he told me too," added Danny.

Both of us at the same time said, "Mark."

"Where are you at?" I asked.

"Were driving home already," Danny replied.

"Okay, I will be there in an hour," I added.

Dayeneliss Perez

I grabbed my office key from my front pocket and unlocked the door, as I was making my way inside, I slowly closed the door behind me and walked to my chair.

"Has Jacob woken up," I asked Danny.

"No, doctors said he's between life and death. He's in really bad shape," Danny replied with a devastated sigh.

As I was hearing what Danny was saying to me, I saw a piece of paper on my desk. I don't remember leaving that there. I moved my chair forward to reach the paper. Held the paper and leaned back to read it. The letter wrote:

Eva Valdez, I know you want to bring Cole back to his precious little family and I can give him to you under the condition that you don't tell anyone about this, and you come alone. Otherwise, there would be serious consequences with this, you don't want me to hurt Cole like I did with Jacob and Shelly. We are meeting at the old, abandoned theater on 13th Street at 3:00 AM. Don't be late or early. If I find out you told someone about this, there will be consequences. I will not hesitate to take Cole's life. I'll be waiting for you.

Sincerely, Mark,

I had a knot in my stomach, how did this paper come here? I had completely forgotten about Dany in the line.

"Hello Eva, are you still there?"

"Yes, I'm here, can I talk to you later Danny," I said trying to maintain my composure.

"No, wait Eva," replied Danny over the phone.

I clicked on the decline button ending the call.

The life of this little boy is in my hands, and this bastard is the one that killed shelly, and left Jacob between life and death and now he has Cole in his hands. Finding him would solve two cases and bring two families at peace. A knocking came from the door.

"Who is it," I called out, quickly folding the paper into smaller pieces putting it in the pocket of my jacket.

"It's me," Josh replied.

"Come in," I responded trying to maintain my cool.

Josh opens the door slowly and enters the room.

He gazed at me for a straight minute frowning his eyebrows.

"You okay, you seem like you have seen a ghost," said Josh, slowly walking towards my desk. My hands were shaking nonstop.

"Yes, I am completely fine," tucking my hands in my pocket so Josh wouldn't notice my trembling fingers.

"Do you need something, Josh?" I asked, putting on a fake smile.

"Yes, Derick wants you in his office. Governor Waltor is there," Josh said, rubbing his hands over his mouth.

"Okay," I replied darting out to the door without making eye contact with Josh.

"What's up with her?" thought Josh in his mind, folding his arms confused by Eva's behavior. Hurrying to Derick's office, I took hold of the doorknob and turned it, pushing the door open. Josh came in after me and closed the door.

Waltor sat at one end of the table. Micheal stood behind the chair across from Waltor. Derick was at the other end, close to Waltor.

"Good evening, Mr. Waltor," I mentioned, as I was walking to take a seat. Micheal drawled the chair out for me.

"Thank you," I said to Micheal. Returning with a smile and a slight nod.

"We have a suspect," I added as I was seating down.

"You do?" asked Derick and Waltor surprised.

"Yes," I replied, not trying to say anything more than I know.

"What's his name?" questioned Derick, standing from his seat eager to know who it is.

"I don't have a name yet," I replied, signaling Josh to not say a word about me knowing anything.

"Then how do you have a suspect if you don't know what's their name?" added Derick.

"I'm still figuring it out," I said. "I promise you, Waltor, your son will be brought back to you, no matter what.""

Waltor remained silent and gave me a slight nod, getting up from his seat and heading out of the office.

Josh was gazing at me with his eyebrows frowned, confused about my behavior. The room was completely quiet after Waltor left.

I looked at my watch, it was 1:45am in the morning,

"I have to go," I said, pushing my seat back, heading towards the door.

Hologram

As I was about to open the door, Derick called out,

"Eva, if you know something, say it and don't try solving it yourself remember that we work as a team."

"Yea," I whispered and exit the room. I know I can't tell them about the letter,

Cole's life is in between; I can't let Mark hurt Cole.

Derick looked at Josh,

"Do you know something?"

"No," Josh quickly responded, walking out to the door to catch up to Eva.

I was rushing out of the station till I heard Josh's voice behind me.

CHAPTER 23

I pulled the car door open, making my way in. As I was going to close the door Josh came and held it.

"Why did you lie back there?" questioned Josh. "You do know his name, you were about to tell me back in the hospital," he added.

"Josh, I can't explain right now," I said, removing his jacket and giving it back to him. "Here, I have a spare one in the car, thank you," I said closing the door, backing up the car and driving out onto the road.

Josh stood there watching as Eva drove off. He puts his Jacket on; it had the aroma of Eva. He walks back inside the police station. Heading to his office with a frown face, Micheal saw him from a distance and rushed and entered inside Josh's office.

"What's up with Eva?" asked Micheal placing the chair out for him to seat.

"I'm not sure, but she's definitely up to something," Josh replied. He leaned back in his chair and slipped his hands into his pockets. Josh felt something in his right pocket. He takes it out, it's a note. He unfolded it. It was a handwritten letter; this caught Josh's attention, and he began to read it.

"What does it say?" asked Micheal curious.

Josh finished reading it and stayed silent, with his hand over his mouth shocked by what he had read.

"What is it?" asked Micheal worried.

Josh didn't reply he remained quiet. Micheal grabbed the paper out of Josh's hand and began to read it.

"That's why Eva was so anxious to leave because she has to meet up with this guy," Josh said, worried, slamming his hands on the desk and standing up from his seat.

"Did Eva left already?" asked Micheal placing the paper upon the desk.

"Yes," Josh said, glancing at his watch. It was 2:05 AM. "I have to go to the theater." He opened the drawer and grabbed his car keys.

"I'm coming with you," replied Micheal standing up from his chair.

Josh let out a sigh, "Micheal, I think it best for you to go back to your house, you're not even a cop and it's not your responsibility," added Josh.

"I am going whether you like it or not," replied Micheal firmly.

CHAPTER 24

"I'm so exhausted," exclaimed Danny throwing himself on the couch face first.

"Eva!" called out Harry. There was no response in the house. Harry shouted again but still no response.

"She's probably at the police station. You know how she practically lives there," Danny said with a smirk. "I called her earlier, and she said she was there." He stood up from the sofa and walked to the bathroom to shower.

"Okay, did she say that she was on her way," said Harry concern.

"She told me about an hour, but I don't know how long because she basically left me there talking by myself," Danny responded closing the bathroom door behind him.

Harry goes to his bathroom and takes a shower to give Eva some time to come home.

After Danny finishes taking a shower, he goes to put his sleep pants on and goes directly to bed.

After Harry finishes his shower, he checks the time. It's 2:24 AM, and Eva still hasn't come home. He calls her phone, but it goes straight to voicemail. He calls again but no answer. Harry then gives Josh a call.

Josh is driving to the theater and hears his phone ringing, he checks his screen to see the caller, it is Harry.

"Damn it!" Josh exclaimed, "he is going to ask about Eva."

Micheal inhaled a deep breath in, "say that she will be staying at your place tonight," replied Micheal.

"He won't believe me, plus they would probably even show up to my place, and then when they find out that I'm actually not there, nor Eva, they'll kill me,"

"Then say that you don't know where she's at," added Micheal.

Josh nodded, "no, I'm just not going to answer," Josh said placing his phone on silent and placing it on the cupholders of the center console of the car. Harry calls again, and again. Until he stopped and send message. The message read, "Josh, please give me a call when you can it's about Eva."

Josh didn't reply nor saw the message for it to not be seen as read.

"They're worried about Eva," replied Micheal.

"You don't think I know that" replied Josh upset. Josh parks the car on the side of the road across the end of the theatre, shutting the car off. There was a moment of silence for a few minutes in the car.

"I have to apologize for earlier, I shouldn't had punch you out of my own rage, I don't know what I was thinking. I thought you were the one behind all this," Josh said.

"Don't worry about it, I accept your apology," replied Micheal with a smile, taking out a gps tracker from his leather bag.

"What are you going to do with that?" asked Josh curious looking at Micheal.

"I'm going to place it under their vehicle since they'll meet Eva here. Then, when they drive off, we'll know their location," Micheal said, grinning.

"Good idea," replied Josh.

"If this Bastard thinks that he is ahead of us, were going to be not one step ahead but two," noted Micheal.

They both noticed Eva driving up. She parked her car by the road, got out, and rushed into the old, abandoned theater. She kept looking around to check if anyone was nearby. Making her way in.

"I'm going in," said Josh opening his door, "stay here," he added quietly closing the door, running after Eva.

After Josh entered the theater, Michael carefully got out of the car. He rushed to the only other vehicle parked nearby: a black Cadillac. Micheal casually walked beside it like normal and looked at his surroundings. Micheal glanced at the windows to check if there was anyone inside, there was no one in the car. He quickly places the GPS tracker under the Cadillac, then casually walks back to the car.

CHAPTER 25

It has been years since Josh had placed a foot in this theatre, he would come on the weekends sneaking through the back doors to watch a movie. Now, he is coming in again not to watch a movie but to be in a thriller himself. Eva still hasn't noticed that he was following her. Josh rapidly grabbed Eva from behind, placing his hand over her mouth for her not to make single noise moving her to a corner. I was so scared, my heart was pounding so fast, until I heard a whisper in my ear, "shhh," it sounded like Josh's voice. I turned around to face the person, and it was Josh.

"What are you doing here," I whispered, trying to avoid the fact that we were so close together like never before.

"I should be asking you the same thing. Why didn't you warn anyone? I wasn't going to let you do this alone. It's dangerous," Josh said quietly.

"How did you know I'll be here?" I asked.

"You left the note in my Jacket," Josh replied, taking the note out of his pocket showing me.

"I'm so stupid," I responded.

"No, I am glad that you left it in my Jacket because if not no one would know where you could have been, your brothers are worried about you."

"I know, but I need to go save Cole, the same thing is not going to happen again with what happened with Shelly," I said trying to leave from Josh.

He held me and didn't let me go.

"You're not going to go over there," exclaimed Josh quietly.

Josh and I saw Mark with Cole next to him from a distance.

"I have to go, he's there," I whispered, anxiously trying to go to Cole.

Josh held me tighter from escaping. After waiting a minute with Josh not letting me go. We can hear Mark angry at me by not appearing on time. Suddenly, Cole disappears in a second. Josh and I took a closer look, confused. Then saw a remote on Marks right hand. We both looked at each other, both of us whispering at the same, "it's a hologram."

A women figure appeared in the dark walking up to Mark.

"She hasn't come Carmen!" yelled Mark angrily to Carmen.

"She always keeps her word with everything, she must be here any time now," responded Carmen nervously.

"She hasn't arrived in these 5 minutes that we have waited, and I specifically told her not to come early nor late, she's testing my patience, we are leaving because she's probably getting backup to build a trap to catch us," said Mark.

"Carmen is with him," I whispered to myself shock. She has been the one warning him all this time, how couldn't I have seen it earlier. I slowly stepped back, causing a loud cracking noise; Mark heard it.

"Find her she is in here somewhere," commanded Mark to his men's.

He quickly scanned the theatre from up to bottom and side to side. Caught Josh's shadow and mine.

"THERE!" shouted Mark pointing to our direction.

Before we could have escape in a second, the man electrocuted Josh from behind. Josh fell to the ground; I held him to prevent him from getting hurt by the fall.

"We found her," called out the man, but before I could have escape the man tasered me. I felt this heavy shock that numbed my whole body, but the shock wasn't that rough on me like it was on Josh. I could hear Mark's voice from a distance, I felt so weak, I couldn't feel an ich of my body nor move a muscle.

"I told you she would have come," Carmen said, after the men's found Eva. Mark walked up to me and bent his knees.

"Look what you made me do," he said with an unpleasant smirk.

My eyes begin too slowly close.

"Pick her up," commanded Mark.

The men picked Eva's body and looked over at Josh lying on the ground.

"What do you want to do with him?" asked the men carrying Eva in his arms.

"Leave him here, I don't care," responded Mark, walking out of the theatre.

CHAPTER 26

Micheal glanced at the time; the time read 3:14.

"Why have they taken so long, what happened," spoke Micheal worried.

Suddenly, a man exits the theatre carrying a woman in his arms, Micheal takes a closer look to see who it was.

"It's Eva, they have Eva."

Then he saw another man coming out with another women walking besides him, Micheal recognized her face.

"Carmen!" exclaimed Micheal shocked.

They all entered the black Cadillac and rapidly left but Micheal had placed the GPS tracker under the vehicle, so they can leave wherever they want their location is being tracked. Still no sign of Josh though.

After they left Micheal opened the car door and ran inside the theatre searching for Josh.

"Josh!" shouted Micheal, looking all over the theater. After a minute of searching and calling Josh, he encounters Josh lying on the floor behind a column, mumbling Eva's name.

"Josh, what the hell happened?" asked Micheal trying to lift him up.

Josh was extremely weak to get up from all the electricity his body received. The only thing Josh said was,

"They took Eva," barely having energy, then slowly closing his eyes.

"No, no, no," Micheal said stuttering, gently slapping Josh's face for him to remain awake.

"Talk to me, Josh!"

Micheal quickly draws out his cell phone from his back pocket and dialed 911.

"I have an officer down; I need an ambulance NOW!"

"Okay, where is your location?" asked the women on the other side of the line.

"Were in the old, abandoned theater on 13th street," replied Micheal.

"Okay, were sending help right away," added the women.

"Thank you," replied Micheal tucking his cell back to his pocket.

After 7 minutes waiting Micheal can hear the siren of the ambulance nearby. Two paramedics came rushing inside the theatre.

"Here!" shouted Micheal waving his hands in the air for the paramedics to notice where he was at. The two paramedics rushed to his direction pushing a stretcher, carrying Josh to it. One of the paramedics checked his pulse, while the other was checking Josh's breathing.

"What happened to him?" asked the paramedic checking his pulse.

"I don't know," replied Micheal, looking at both of the paramedics.

Pushing the stretcher to the ambulance. Micheal also hoped in the back. Micheal observed how the paramedic were doing their work. Everything was at fast pace, but everything was going slow pace for Micheal. Eva has been captured by Mark, now Josh is in these conditions, Harry and Danny are worried about their sister, everything is a complete disaster.

"Could this get any worse," whispered Micheal under his breath.

"Let's just pray that he lives," responded the paramedic in a worried tone.

"What do you mean by that?" questioned Micheal gripping on the grey steel handle inside the ambulance.

"He looks like someone hit him hard with the taser." That could have serious effects," the paramedic said, continuing to help Josh with his medical needs.

"Why were you two in that abandoned theatre, no one goes there anymore?" asked the paramedic raising an eyebrow.

"He was after Eva because she was going to meet with the kidnappers of Cole and he wanted to protect her and I guess the person tasered him or electrocuted him with something, I don't know I wasn't there; I was in the car, then I entered inside because he was taking too long and that's when I encountered him almost dying," responded Micheal letting out a devasted sigh.

CHAPTER 27

I woke up, I was lying on a black leather sofa looking around in the room where it was an office, then I encountered Carmen and Mark next to me. I slowly got up from the sofa to sit. They both looked at me. I searched for my gun, but it was gone.

"I have it," called out Mark with a grin, coming closer to me.

"Why are you doing this?" I asked softly, not to pull a trigger because he seems like a type of guy that gets fired up easily. Glancing at Mark then at Carmen. My body still felt a numbing tingle from the taser.

"Why did you brought Josh, if we specifically told you to not bring nobody," Mark said irritated.

"I didn't bring him, he brought himself because he saw the note you gave me," I responded, putting my wrists in fists, ready to knock Mark down.

"Take her!" shouted Mark, noticing that Eva was going to fire at him.

The man grabbed me from my back and throwed me across the cold floor. I felt lightheaded, wishing for all of this to stop. I slowly got my hands one by one on the floor and noticed drops of blood coming from my lip. Before I could have gotten up the men kicked me on my stomach, making me to fall on my back. That kick made me lose my breath for a straight minute. I began to cough out blood. One kick to the stomach was almost unbearable to resist.

"GET UP!" yelled the man.

I was too weak to get up, my whole body was in pain.

"YOU!" shouted the man in a deep voice, taking me by my shirt and lifting me up. His big, muscled hand was wrapped in a fist, ready to punch me. The grip of his hand on my shirt was so tight.

"I don't want her killed," commanded Mark, walking behind the man.

"Don't you think she has done enough," replied the man angry. "We were almost caught."

"Yes, I know, but I want to do something to her before I kill her," said Mark with a smirk.

"Take her to the Lab," added Mark.

"NO!" I shouted dragging my feet on the floor, while the man was pushing me.

Carmen was standing there watching as they were dragging Eva out of the office. She began to feel some regret in her heart from what she did to Eva because she was the one that left that note on her desk.

Hitting my elbow as hard as I could across the man's stomach to release me from his grip. Escaping away from him.

Suddenly, Mark grabbed me by my arm, tightly holding it and taking out an injection with a clear liquid inside, inserting it on my wrist. Trying to remove my arm from his grip but it was impossible he had more strength than I ever did.

After Mark released my hand, I looked at my wrist and the injection was still attached to my skin, I quickly removed it, but it was too late he placed all the fluid in my body. I looked up at Mark, I began to see two of him. My vision was blurry, shortening of breath. My legs began to feel weak. I had never felt this feeling in my life beside the taser earlier, but this was worser. Eva's balance became unsteady, causing her to fall to her side, but Mark caught her before she hit the floor.

"Unfortunately, you're my enemy because if we met in another circumstances, you could have been my wife because you have all the qualities I want," said Mark, gently brushing his hand across Eva's face. Carmen was behind watching, jealous of the way Mark treated Eva.

"Why are you saying that?" asked Carmen.

"What the true," responded Mark with a smirk on his face.

"You fool! A women beat you up, carry her and take her to the lab," commanded Mark.

The man rushed to carry Eva, embarrassed of the fact that Eva took him down. Taking her to the Lab and placing her onto the chair. Mark reclines the chair back for Eva.

CHAPTER 28

After the ambulance arrived at the hospital Josh began to open his eyes slowly, looking around him.

"What happened!" yelled Josh as he quickly climbed out of the hospital bed.

"Woh! Take it easy," said Micheal, holding him back to lay him down.

"They took Eva, I have to go and find her," responded Josh drowsy.

"We're going to find her, don't worry," replied Micheal, slowly pushing him back to the bed.

Josh was still trying to get his senses back.

"I am going to call Harry," Micheal said, taking out his phone from his back pocket and dialing Harry's number.

"Hello?" Harry answered in a sleepy voice.

"Hey Harry, we need you asap in the hospital," added Micheal, nervously.

"Why, what happened?" Harry replied worried, quickly getting off his bed, putting his shirt on, opening Danny's bedroom door.

"Long story, just come here," responded Micheal.

"Okay, I'll be there," said Harry ending the call.

Harry hurried and removed Danny's sheets off him.

"Danny, hurry we have to go to the hospital, something happened."

"What happened now," Danny said letting out a deep breath, slowly bringing his feet to the side of the bed, half asleep. Danny looked at his nightstand to see what time it was. The clock read 4:05.

"Really," whispered Danny sleepy. Getting up from his bed, putting his shirt on and a pair of blue jeans. Walking out of his room and opening Eva's bedroom door. She wasn't there and the bed was neatly done since the morning; she still hasn't come home. Danny became worried. He hears Harry outside beeping nonstop. Rushing downstairs and putting his shoes on and grabbing his coat from the hanger. Locking the door from the inside, running to the passenger door.

"Eva never arrived home?" asked Danny concerned, "Its 4 in the morning."

"Yea, she didn't arrive, but something happened because Micheal called me worried," added Harry, accelerating the car fast.

CHAPTER 29

Danny and Harry ran inside the hospital. Micheal sees them from the hospital's hallway and whistles to them, waving his hand out for them to see where he was at. Micheal enters to Josh's hospital room with Harry and Danny behind him.

"What happened?" shouted Danny worried.

"Where's Eva?" questioned Harry.

"Eva left to go find Cole, but they took her," replied Josh.

Danny grabbed Josh by his neck and turned his hand into a full firm fist and punched Josh across his mouth.

"Danny Stop it, fighting is not going to solve anything," shouted Harry upset, removing him away from Josh. Causing him to fall to the cold floor.

"Why didn't you warn us about what Eva was going to do," Harry said upset.

"I didn't want to worry you two," replied Josh, covering his mouth with his hand. Blood coming out of his mouth.

"Now we don't know where they took Eva, Damn it!" yelled Danny.

"Carmen is with him, that traitor," whispered Josh angry.

Everyone stayed quiet, completely speechless by what Josh had said.

"Well actually, I placed a gps tracker under their vehicle they left in," Micheal added trying to uplift Harry and Danny with some hope.

"What do you mean Josh?" questioned Harry. Josh took a deep breath before he spoke.

"Carmen and Mark are the ones behind all this," added Josh frustrated. "So, she has been the one telling Mark about where we were going to go and what was our next step," noted Danny, folding his arms together, analyzing all his ideas to a conclusion. Micheal drawled out his phone from his pocket and watched where the tracker was indicting where they took Eva.

"This is their location," Micheal said showing everyone the tracker, pointing at the red dot. Micheal tapped on the red dot indicating their location. An address appeared; he copied and pasted the address on the map to see the distance from the hospital to the house.

"Its 10 minutes away from us now," added Micheal.

'Let's go and get Eva," Josh exclaimed, rushing out of the hospital room. A young nurse was entering while Josh was making his way out. "Where are you going? You can't leave yet, Josh. You're not discharged," she said, holding a clipboard with papers.

"I have to go, it's an emergency," replied Josh, leaving the hospital. The other three followed Josh and left the hospital room rushing out. The nurse was confused about why they were all leaving in such a hurry. Josh waited outside beside Harry's car because he left his in the theater. Harry unlocked the car making his way to it.

Dayeneliss Perez

Harry took the wheel, Josh settled into the passenger seat, while Danny and Michael took their seats in the backseat. Micheal gave his phone to Josh to have it up front for Harry to follow the tracker.

CHAPTER 30

Everyone was silent till they arrived at the location. Harry turned the headlights off. Slowly parking the car to a nearby bush where you can't see it from the house. Josh looks outside and sees only the rooftop of the house.

"Says it's here," Harry said raising an eyebrow, seeing the tracker.

"Okay, then let's go in," Josh said, placing bullets into his handgun.

"Have you ever shotten before?" questioned Danny to Micheal.

"A few times when I used to hunt with my dad," replied Micheal.

"Okay, here," Danny replied handing him a handgun, "It has the lock off," added Danny.

"Okay," replied Micheal as he took it, his hand trembling as he touched the handgun.

Everyone exited the car and quietly approached the house.

"We have to separate," said Harry.

"Alright, Josh and Michael, you two go in the front. Danny and I will take the back. This way, it'll be easier," said Harry.

Harry and Danny walked to the back of the house, while Josh and Micheal went to the front door. Micheal grabbed the doorknob, but it was locked.

Dayeneliss Perez

"It's locked," said Micheal looking at Josh who was staring at him with a face that read, "are you stupid."

"Of course, it's going to be locked, did you really thought they would have their front door opened," added Josh.

"No, but how are we going to get in?" asked Micheal.

"Like this," replied Josh hitting the doorknob with the grip module of his handgun. The doorknob fell to the floor with the third hit. Josh looked at Micheal who was surprised on how the doorknob fell. Josh slowly swung the door open and quietly enters in with Micheal following behind him. The house inside was a regular home, he could hear voices from a distance, everything was clear where they were standing. Josh and Micheal walked to the far end hallway.

Josh and Micheal continue to walk the hallway till they reached an open room. There was Mark standing and Eva sitting on the chair reclined back unconsciously.

"Eva!" yelled Josh, carrying her in his arms. Mark quickly turned around to face them and saw that Micheal was already pointing the gun at him.

"How did you make your way in?" questioned Mark angry.

"By the front door, what did you think," Micheal added with a sarcastic grin. Josh looks at Eva and sees her wrist with stitches.

"What did you do to her!" exclaimed Josh furious.

"A little something," replied Mark with a smirk.

"How cute! The two-prince charming's rescuing the princess," Mark said mocking, holding the remote in his hand. "If one of you two move, all you're going to cause is more trouble, you see this remote right," moving the remote in the air. "it's connected to the chip Eva has in her wrist and every time I press on the button the weaker she becomes and slowly causing her to die."

Danny and Harry made their way into the house. The back door was unlocked so it was easier for them to enter. Harry and Danny went upstairs; the voices began to sound closer with every step they took up. Harry indicates to Danny to be silent by placing his finger on his lips. Danny returned with a slight nod. Harry slowly leans his back on the wall and slide to the corner of the wall to see if there is anyone in the area. There was two men speaking to one another, they were Mark's bodyguards. Harry scrolled the silencer in his gun, preparing it to action, while Danny was holding his handgun firmly waiting to act.

Carmen slowly appears in the dark behind Micheal. Josh sees her and quickly alerts Micheal.

Micheal hears a trigger of a gun behind him

"Behind you Micheal!" shouted Josh.

Micheal quickly turns around and shoots Carmen on her right thigh and at that same moment Micheal fires, Carmen shoots Micheal in his hand where he was holding his handgun. Causing his gun to fall onto the floor. Carmen falls to the floor aching in pain. Micheal looks at his hand, covered in his own blood.

Dayeneliss Perez

"I don't know whether to look at it or not," Micheal asked himself.

Micheal takes out his long sleeve shirt leaving him wearing his white tank top and wraps his wounded hand, while placing pressure onto it. Gunshots start to fire one after the other.

"Go to them," said Harry signaling downstairs.

Danny rushed downstairs running straightly to where he heard the gunshots.

One of the men went to go downstairs, Harry without hesitation pulled the trigger, hitting the man on his chest. Harry rushed up and shoots the other man on his right knee. The men shouted in pain, holding his knee. Harry grabbed him from his hair and pulled him up with a sharp knife against his throat.

"If you don't do as I say, this precious knife is going to be cutting through your neck," mentioned Harry. "Where is Cole?" he added.

The man automatically listened and showed Harry the way. Harry was worried about the others who could have those gunshots gone to.

"There behind that door, that's where Cole is at," the man said pointing at the door. Harry came to a stop to it, trying to open the door but it was locked.

"Give me the keys," said Harry angry.

The man nervously shaking taking out the chain of keys in his pocket. Shakily, going through the chain of keys, picking the key to open the door.

"Here," handing Harry the key.

Hologram

Harry took the key and unlocked the door. Sliding it open there he saw Cole on the cold floor lying. Harry brought the man in the room, throwing him against the ground and rushing to Cole. The man quietly took out his gun from his back and shoots Harry in his left side of his stomach before he can grab Cole.

"Damn it!" exclaimed Harry, looking at his gunshot wound. He quickly took out his handgun and shot the man in the forehead, dropping him dead on the floor.

Harry shirt was getting stained with his blood. Harry brings his phone out and calls 911 and tells them that they have found Cole and that he has been shot. He carried Cole and took him out of the room and slowly walked to where the others were at. It was getting difficult to breathe for Harry, but he got the few strength he had to carry Cole.

Suddenly, Danny appears in the room.

"Don't mess with my sister!" Danny shouted as he pulled the trigger. The bullet hit Mark's heart, and he collapsed to the ground. The remote in his hand fell on the floor, breaking into small pieces.

Micheal took a sigh of relief that Mark was dead, but his hand was in so much pain. He faced Carmen, who was groaning in pain by the shot in her right thigh. She was bleeding heavily.

"Please help me!" cried out Carmen in pain holding onto her gunshot wound. The sound of police sirens was outside of the house.

"Who called 911?" asked Josh.

"Me,'" replied Harry weak, with Cole in his arms.

"You got shot," said Danny concerned rushing to his direction to get Cole from his arms.

"Yea," replied Harry placing his hand on the wound.

The police officers emerged in the house.

"Everything is settled but we all need to go to the hospital," Micheal said sarcastically.

"You though need a lesson taught," Micheal said grabbing Carmen by her hair and dragging her out of the house.

"Let me go Jerk!" yelled Carmen leaving a trace of blood from her thigh. Two officers helped Harry out of the house because he was too weak and pale from the gunshot wound. Josh carried Eva out of the house, rushing her to the ambulance and Danny did the same with Cole. All the officers were in shock by Cole's appearance. The paramedics took them all to the hospital except for Danny and Josh. They both drove in the car; they parked by the bush. Carmen was in the ambulance with a police officer at all times watching her. The drive with Danny and Josh was quiet, no one said a word about anything till they arrived at the hospital. They brought Harry down from the ambulance, rushing him into the emergency unit. The gunshot wound had worsened. Danny and Josh rushed out of the car, running to the paramedics that were taking Harry in.

"Will he be, okay?" asked Danny worried.

"We are trying our best Danny," replied the paramedic.

Danny and Josh watched how they were taking one by one inside. After they placed everyone in the hospital, they brought Carmen down. Danny couldn't stand her alive while his siblings were in the hospital because of her fault. He went to her, grabbed her by her hair and got her out of the paramedic stretcher. Putting his hand into a firm fist and punched her across her face. Danny has never laid hands on a woman before, but Carmen messed with his sibling's, and he was not going to stand there and watch her. Before he could have punch her again the police officers removed him off her.

"If Harry and Eva don't make it out alive, I am going to kill you!" shouted Danny, watching as they take Carmen inside with her nose bleeding. Josh places his hand on Danny's shoulder. Danny looks at Josh, then heads inside the hospital.

"Danny wait, don't do anything that you'll regret," said Josh following him inside.

"Don't worry Josh, I am not I am going to see Eva and Harry," replied Danny going to the receptionist. Josh let out a sigh of relief because he thought Danny was going to do something to Carmen.

"What room is Eva and Harry Vasquez, I'm their brother," asked Danny trying to remain calm.

"Your name?" asked the receptionist.

"Danny Vasquez," replied Danny, leaning onto the countertop.

"Danny they are both on surgery rooms at the moment, you can see them when the procedure is done," she responded.

Dayeneliss Perez

"Do you know how long that would take?" asked Danny overwhelmed with the whole situation.

"I'm sorry but I can't give you a time for sure," she said.

"Okay, thank you though," replied Danny as he walked directly to the waiting room. Josh followed him. Danny's back rested against the cool wall by the large windows. He stared out to the hospital's garden. He sat down on the ground, feeling the weight of the moment settle around him. The light from the sun slowly started to rise.

CHAPTER 31

"Hey, Josh," called out Elizabeth walking to his direction.

"Hey," replied Josh upset.

"Jacob woke up," added Elizabeth with joy in her eyes.

"That's amazing," Josh responded trying to be enthusiastic but the only person that was in his mind was Eva.

"Is everything good?" questioned Elizabeth her smile slowly fading away.

"Not really," replied Josh looking at Danny's direction. Elizabeth turned to face, and saw Danny sitting against the wall, unhappy, almost seeming weak.

"What happened?" asked Elizabeth concerned.

"Long story, Eva and Harry are right now in the surgery rooms because Harry got shot and Mark did something to Eva, but the good thing is that Cole is found and the bastard that shot your cousin is dead," Josh replied trying to sound uplifting.

"I'm going to go and talk with Danny," Elizabeth said placing her hand on Josh's shoulder then leaving to Danny's direction.

Elizabeth stood beside Danny; he slowly brought his eyes to meet hers. Elizabeth saw the sorrow through Danny's eyes. She sat down next to Danny giving him a warm smile.

Dayeneliss Perez

"You and your siblings are one of the most courageous people I have ever met."

Danny remained silent with a warm smile. He looked down at his hands with spots of blood stained. Elizabeth stood up and left. After a little while Elizabeth returned back handing him a bottle of water.

"Thanks," Danny said quietly.

"You should get rest," Elizabeth added gazing at his eyes. Danny took a sip of his water.

"I can't leave Harry and Eva here, I'm going to wait for them," replied Danny.

"Okay, I understand but how many hours did you get of rest?" questioned Elizabeth.

"I don't know," Danny said shrugging his shoulders.

"Okay," whispered Elizabeth sitting next to him and placed her hand on his. Danny was surprised. Her warm, soft hands rested upon his, with her nails painted cherry red. He placed his other hand on top of hers and gently rubbed his finger on her hand. He turns to meet her eyes, there was something about Elizabeth that no other girl has, it's almost feels like he knows her from another life, her eyes, her lips, everything. She was the women that Danny has ever dreamed of. He felt peace when she was around even though the situation was hard to handle.

CHAPTER 32

After the procedure was done, removing the bullet in Harry's body. After a few minutes, Harry opened his eyes. He still felt the effects of the anesthesia. When he saw Olivia, he held her hand and whispered as high as his sore, weak body allowed him, "Would you marry me?"

Olivia stared at Harry, surprised but happy. She giggled as she watched him act silly from the anesthesia.

Then suddenly I began to open my eyes and encountered myself in a hospital bed, my right wrist was wrapped. The last thing I remember was Mark injecting me, other than that my memory was gone. What even happened, everything was so peaceful here right now. The doctor came into the room with Danny following him. I was so relieved to see Danny here.

"I'll leave you two alone," said the doctor leaving.

"Eva!" shouted Danny with excitement running to me, wrapping his arms around me, and giving me a tight hug.

"Danny I am so happy to see you," I replied, giving him one last squeeze.

"Where's Harry?" I asked.

"Oh, he got shot, but he is fine though. He's in the recovery room at the moment, I was actually on my way to see him," Danny replied with a slight smile.

"By whom?' I questioned concerned.

"By one of the guys of Mark," replied Danny, "How do you feel," asked Danny.

"Oh, I'm fine don't worry, go and check on him," I said with a slight nervous smile.

"Okay," Danny said leaving the hospital room. After Danny left there was a knock at the door.

"Come in," I called out. The door slowly opened, it was Josh. He walked in and closed the door behind him and walked to me.

"How are you feeling?" he asked.

"I'm good," I replied with a big smile, "you can sit here if you like," I said patting the side of the bed.

"Okay," Josh replied sitting on the bed., "You should have told one of us though when you were leaving to the theatre to meet up with Mark," added Josh quite upset.

"I know," I replied turning my face down. "How is Cole?" I asked. He gently placed his hand under my chin, lifting my face to his, and in that moment, the world seemed to pause.

"Eva, I can't bear the thought of losing you. You're my everything," he murmured, his voice filled with sincerity. Those words made my pulse race. In that very moment nothing else seemed to matter but me and him. His eyes would bring me to another dimension. The doctor entered the room.

"Alright, I need a moment to speak with Eva," the doctor said, his smile directed at Josh. Josh gently held my hand, kissing it softly. "I'll be outside if you need anything," he said, his fingers gently brushing through my hair before he turned to leave.

"Everything seems to be good, how are you feeling?" he asked.

"I feel good," I replied.

"Okay, just sign these papers, and you'll be set for discharge," he said, handing me the clipboard. I stared at the papers and began to fill them out.

CHAPTER 33

After a long tough few days, Cole was reunited with his family. Derick spoke to the news reporters that were asking him about the kidnapping of Cole and how he was found.

"The true heroes who rescued Cole are Harry, Danny, Eva, Josh, and Michael. They are the best cops in this department," Derick said, placing his hand on Danny's and Harry's shoulders.

They both returned with a smile. Solving Cole's case also helped solve Shelly's case. I needed to tell Mrs. Cruz that they had found and killed her daughter's murderer. This news might bring her some comfort after her loss.

Danny came beside me and whispered, "Do you think Mr. Waltor is going to pay us the money he promised in the beginning?"

I sighed and rolled my eyes, expressing my disbelief, "Danny, are you serious?""

The news reporter began to circle around us. I wasn't in the mood to speak to any reporters or answer any questions. Mr. Waltor made his way in the circle that surrounded us with reporters.

He took the microphone and said, "I'm very thankful for these officers for bringing my son home. Please give them some privacy. I'm sure they're tired, so let's not overwhelm them with questions. I really appreciate it. Thank you.""

All the reporters began to pick up their equipment and walk to their vehicles. Mr. Waltor wouldn't stop thanking us. His smile wouldn't fade, and his eyes were glimmering with joy.

"I am going to give you the money I promised," added Mr. Waltor.

Danny looked at me with his eyes wide open and with a bright smile that was screaming excitement all over his face. Harry sat across from us. He heard the announcement while still healing from his gunshot wound. Mr. Waltor stopped in front of me, "can I give you a hug Eva." I smiled and nodded, opening my hands wide. Mr. Waltor gave me a big squeeze and whispered, "thank you."

I felt so happy and fulfilled when a child was brought back to their family. Cole came running to Harry, who was sitting giving him a big hug. Mr. Waltor continued talking about the money he was going to give. I left everyone and went to my car. Driving to Mrs. Cruz place. Pulling up at her driveway, her front porch was surrounded with beautiful bright colored flowers in pots. Getting out of the car and approaching her front door. I drew my hand and began to knock. After a few seconds Mrs. Cruz pulled the door open. Her eyes were wide open, surprised by my appearance.

"Hello Eva," she said in a gentle voice. She looked at my wrapped wrist and asked me, "What had happened?""

I let out a laugh, "long story," I replied placing my hand behind me.

Dayeneliss Perez

"I came here because they found your daughter Shelly's killer. His name is Mark. My brother, Harry shot him. He also captured Governor Waltor's youngest son and held him for days."

"Oh dear," Mrs. Cruz replied with her eyes tearing up, choking on her own words, "is he okay," she asked.

I gave a brief nod and responded in a gentle tone, "yes, he is with his family now.""

"Oh!" she cried out relief, breaking in tears.

"Would you like to come in and drink some tea?" asked Mrs. Cruz.

"Yes, I would love too," I replied, making my way in her house.

For a complete list of books by

<u>Dayeneliss Perez</u>

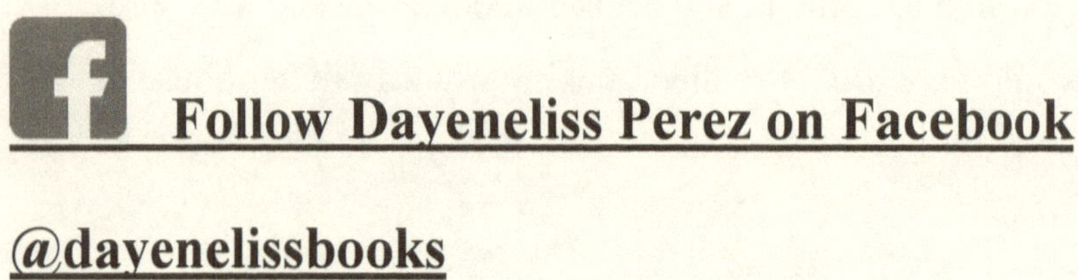

<u>Follow Dayeneliss Perez on Facebook</u>

<u>@dayenelissbooks</u>

<u>Follow Dayeneliss Perez on Instagram</u>

<u>@dayenelissbooks</u>

Dayeneliss Perez lives in the Sunshine State and is the Eldest from her siblings. Daughter to Cuban Parents. She has always been driven to books and writing. All her writings are a little piece of her imagination. She loves nature and has a weakness for Scottish Castles.